ALPHA'S SECRET BABY

WEREBEARS OF GLACIER BAY

MEG RIPLEY

Copyright © 2018 by Meg Ripley
www.redlilypublishing.com

All rights reserved. Printed in the United States of America. No part of this book may be used or reproduced in any manner whatsoever without written permission except in the case of brief quotations embodied in critical articles or reviews.

This book is a work of fiction. Names, characters, businesses, organizations, places, events and incidents either are the product of the author's imagination or are used fictitiously. Any resemblance to actual persons, living or dead, events, or locales is entirely coincidental.

Disclaimer

This book is intended for readers age 18 and over. It contains mature situations and language that may be objectionable to some readers.

CONTENTS

ALPHA'S SECRET BABY

1. Cooper	3
2. Alexis	12
3. Cooper	18
4. Alexis	25
5. Alexis	37
6. Cooper	42
7. Cooper	50
8. Alexis	60
9. Cooper	68
10. Alexis	77
11. Alexis	88
12. Cooper	97
13. Alexis	108
14. Cooper	116
15. Alexis	123
16. Alexis	131
17. Cooper	140
18. Alexis	152
19. Cooper	155

ALPHA'S SECRET BABY

WEREBEARS OF GLACIER BAY

1
COOPER

I spread my paws, running as fast as I could for a time to stretch my muscles and feel every inch of my ursine body. Running on the rocky, hard ground of Glacier Bay National Park would be painful on human feet, but on tough bear paws, it was no concern; my animal form was made for that climate. As I ran, the sun peeked over the Fairweather Range. The golden rays of light did nothing to outshine the blinding whites and vivid glacier blues surrounding me. With so much snow and ice nearby, the landscape itself took on a chilly demeanor. But I knew the warmth of the park firsthand; the heart of its ecosystem, the way in which all wildlife worked together in harmony—or at least, mostly.

As the head Ranger of the park, my job was to maintain that harmony. If something got out of whack—too many mountain goats and not enough wolves, for instance—it could throw the whole ecosystem off. I wasn't so prideful as to think I played a role in Mother Nature's grand design, but it was still my job to do my part there in Glacier Bay, making sure that harmony remained intact to the best of my ability.

My goal for that morning, however, was to keep things harmonious within my clan. I didn't make a habit of being gone for extended periods of time; I hadn't even vacationed for more than a long weekend in years. So, my leaving the park for a week was somewhat of a rare event, and I needed to make sure they were ready.

As I neared the cabin we often met at, I reached out with my mind to see if the others had shifted yet.

Anyone there? I signaled to them.

On my way, Boss. That was Max, my third in command.

Right behind him. Carson, my second.

Once I'd arrived, I shifted back to my human form. Most of us were so used to each other by then that being naked around one another didn't much phase us. Even still, most of us planned to bring clothes when we knew we'd be shifting. I kept clothing everywhere—in my car's trunk, my office, and even there at the cabin. Many of us did, so I dressed and waited for their arrival, looking over the cabin to make sure everything was well.

It wasn't a big place, but the log house had a great room, perfect for gatherings with a large fireplace at one end. It was somewhat of a clan hangout or clubhouse, if we had such a thing. Meetings were held there, events, and whatever else we thought of that required a shelter in the woods, deep in Glacier Bay.

Carson walked through the door first.

"You caught up," I observed.

He harrumphed. "Like it's hard to catch slow-poke McGee." He jerked his thumb in the direction Max would be running from.

Max wasn't far behind him, though, and rushed in, breathless and naked. "Did you take a shortcut or something?" he demanded.

Carson shook his head.

Max growled and yanked a shirt over his head. "Whatever."

"So." I rubbed my hands together. "That brings us to why we're here. I'm going to need the two of you to get along for just this week. Can you handle that?"

"We always get along," Carson said.

"Yeah, as long as I'm losing." Max flung his arm around Carson's neck and tried to playfully choke him, but Carson easily broke free of the hold.

"Why do you even bother?" Carson mocked.

Max rolled his eyes, but got in a cheap shot to Carson's gut when he wasn't looking. Carson acted like he didn't notice, but as I opened my mouth to continue speaking, Carson smacked Max on the back of the head.

"Do I need to separate you two?" I asked.

Max laughed and took a seat. "Just having a little fun."

"I'll only be gone for a week, but that's starting to feel like too long," I said.

I knew when I chose the two of them for their positions, they didn't quite get along. I had stupidly assumed that making them both leaders in the clan would force them to work together. Instead, I'd created a lifelong hassle of keeping the two of them from killing each other.

"I need to know you'll work together," I demanded. "And that I'll be coming back to find everything just as it should be."

"Cooper," Carson said sternly. "You have nothing to worry about with me in charge."

"Hey, I'm in charge, too, dildo," Max added.

"But I'm the second and you're the third."

With that, Max rushed at Carson, putting his head at his chest, trying to tackle him to the ground.

I decided to ignore their antics and just keep talking. "As I was saying, I'll need to know you won't be tearing each other apart. I've even gone as far as to put Jace on duty as backup. If he reports there were issues, I will reconsider my promotion of you both."

That stopped them in their tracks.

Max stood up and shoved Carson aside, who shook his head and straightened his shirt.

"That's not necessary," Carson said. "You know it's just for fun."

"Yeah, we actually do love each other." Max threw his arm around Carson's neck again to bring him into a rough hug and Carson rubbed his knuckles on Max's head until he broke free.

"I am going to be training a whole crop of new Rangers," I went on. "I just may start recruiting. Wouldn't be bad to have some fresh blood in the clan."

Carson put on his serious face. "What is your goal number of clanmates?"

"I don't have a goal. Just talking."

"We could use a few more *ladies*," Max said.

"So could all of Alaska," Carson added.

I nodded. "Then maybe it's time we reach out a bit and network. A lot of us are single and at the age that we're starting to look to settle down. We may have to look hard to find that special lady."

"I may have found her last night," Carson added with a grin.

"No way, that hottie from the bar?" Max asked.

Carson kept grinning and Max sulked.

"I bought her like three drinks," Max mumbled.

"I know." Carson chuckled. "Thanks for that, by the way."

Max grumbled something under his breath.

"Anyhow," I continued, "I'll be gone for a week. It's my job to entice these Rangers not only to make Alaska their home, but also to join as cruise ship tour guides."

"Ah, the dream of all park Rangers everywhere," Max said sarcastically.

I shrugged. "I've never been on a cruise. Could be interesting."

"Yeah, but they don't even leave the boat!" Max threw up his hands in outrage. "What's the point?"

"To stay warm, I'm sure," Carson added.

"Maybe that's something I'll learn more about. Maybe it's just too tricky to have a cruise ship of people come into the park at once. Think about what it would be like to have several thousand people suddenly converge on us for a day at a time."

Max nodded slowly. "You're right. Keep them on the boat."

"Is there anything specific you need me to do this week?" Carson asked.

"You know what needs to be done. Handle anything that comes up as I would, and if you're not sure, reach out to me if it's important, or wait until I get back."

"I'm sure anything that comes up will not be a problem," Carson added.

I checked my watch. "Right. I'm counting on you two."

Max put his hand on my shoulder. "So, do we get t-shirts that say, 'My alpha went on a cruise and all I got was this dumb shirt'?"

I rolled my eyes. "I'll see what I can do." I checked my watch again, then unhooked it and slid it into my bag as I undressed. "Time for me to get going."

Carson and Max stripped as well.

"We'll run you a farewell," Carson said.

I walked outside first, carrying my pack on my back so I would still have my things after I shifted back. I stepped outside into the frosty early April air. With a deep breath, I let my body rearrange into my bear form. My bones creaked and moved, my skin stretched, and thick brown fur sprouted out along with my teeth and claws. It used to hurt back when I was younger, like a whole body of sore muscles and breaking bones. But after a few years, that pain faded, and for most of us, shifting became something like a good stretch once we came of age.

My paws hit the stony ground and two other sets hit behind me. I bounded off, and rather than trying to out run each other, Carson and Max stayed in position just behind me. That was the defensive position we always ran in.

I let my gaze drift upward toward the line of mountains ahead of me. In some places, the land was a wall of ice shards, beautiful and deadly at the same time. The water moved over the ice in slick paths, carving new adventures as it ran. Chunks of ice floated along, usually with animals perched atop.

Depending on the size of the ice chunk, it was an everyday occurrence to see a bald eagle perched, watching for fish, or a sea otter out sunning himself. I couldn't imagine living anywhere but there. Sure, it was the only place I'd lived, but still. I felt blessed to call Alaska my home.

As the cruise ship came into view, I ran over to a more private patch of woods. There, my duffel bag waited for me, and I shifted back to my human form and dressed. Carson and Max transformed as well, and when I was ready, I gave them each a brief hug.

"Don't make me worry," I warned. "Please. I haven't had time away since I was a child, and even though I'm technically working this week, I'm hoping the experience will give me a good breather."

"You can count on us." Max saluted and stood straight as a soldier.

"Yeah, that's what I'm afraid of," I chuckled.

"I'll keep him in line," Carson assured me. "Have a good time, Coop."

Max nodded. "Bring back some hotties."

I nodded to them both and turned, dragging my suitcase along the rocks behind me as I made my way to board the ship.

2
ALEXIS

I reached high into the evening air, stretching my body. That time of year, barely April, was already hot in the Everglades. Somehow, Florida managed to have about two days of winter every year, and even then, it was more like a cool breeze. I hadn't really known anything else, though, so the thought of going so far away, to a place so different, terrified me as much as it exhilarated me.

"You packed your heavy jacket, right?" Hailey asked.

I laughed. "You do know it's going to be in the 30s there. I had to buy a proper winter coat."

"Even better. Sweaters? Blankets? Do you have earmuffs and hats?"

"Hail—" I put my hand on her shoulder. "Don't worry. I've got it."

"I second that," Addie said. "We checked over all her things, Googled like crazy, and made sure she'll be warm enough."

"But Alaska?" Hailey whined. "You've chosen the furthest place from here in the entire freaking country!"

"Hey, it could be worse," I pointed out. "I could be moving to China. At least I'm staying in the US."

Hailey blinked at me with a straight face. "Ha. Alaska barely counts as the US anyway. It's so far!"

"I wouldn't be going if it wasn't an amazing job offer."

The cruise ship company was so eager to get new Rangers onboard that they were going to pay me and a group of others to take a cruise, learn about being a Ranger, and get a feel for what it would be like to work there. They wanted to hook us—and I wanted a free vacation, so it seemed like a win-win. And with a stellar job offer on the line, I couldn't go wrong.

I got up from my lawn chair to mingle with my clan and Hailey's. That night was a huge shifter fest of sorts. We had gathered all the bear clans in the area, along with their significant others and children, and came together for a grand picnic. It was also partly a good-bye party since I would be leaving the next day.

When I had circled around and made my way back to my sister, she was still going on about my upcoming trip.

"Look, Lex, Owen agrees. Your home is here, and you shouldn't leave."

"Whoa, whoa." Owen, the Alpha of Hailey's clan, chuckled and held up his hands. "That's not quite what I said. I said, your home will always be here, as in, you will always have a place to return to. Not that she shouldn't leave if she wants to." He gave Hailey a stern look.

"I might hate it," I said.

"Oh, please." Hailey rolled her eyes. "You've been dying to get out of Florida since you had your first geography lesson in grade school. I knew you'd be gone someday, I just didn't think it'd be so soon after college."

"And you were hoping she'd meet someone here and find a reason to stay," Addie added.

Hailey shushed her. "Of course I want what's best for you, Lex. I just want that to be close to me."

"You know I'm going to miss you like crazy, right?" I said. "My whole life is here, despite whatever wanderlust I've had over the years. Our family, my clan, your clan, which is practically a second clan to me. Owen's right; I have lots of reasons to come back. And besides, the Alaska thing isn't for sure. This is just a chance for me to go there and see it, have a nice little—paid for, by the way—vacation to see if it's something I want to do. Maybe I won't even like it. I'm only—"

"Exploring your options. I know. You've said that so many times, I think you almost believe it."

"I do because it's the truth."

"Come on, you're gonna love it," Hailey accused. "I've seen the photos. I love it, too!"

"Then you can come visit all you want."

"Hey!" She jumped up suddenly and looked around. "Are there crocodiles in Alaska?" She jumped off her seat and charged through the woods, calling out for her boyfriend, Adam, who was a croc shifter.

I looked at Addie and Owen and shrugged. "I don't think Adam would leave Florida."

"Doubt it," Addie confessed.

I let my mind wander for a time. Maybe it would be too much. I'd never been far away from home for a long time. I'd planned to use college as an escape and to get out of the state, but Florida happened to have the best program for a wannabe wildlife conservationist. So I stayed, though on campus so I could at least pretend I wasn't still close to home.

I might miss them all too much. Having a clan was like having a lot of family living nearby, except you were closer, in most cases. Anyone who could actually hear my thoughts when we were in bear form knew far more about me than I cared to let them know. It created a sort of intimacy that all clans understood and experienced. They were closer than siblings or parents, and depending on the age of my clanmate, sometimes he or she functioned in all those roles.

But, as I told Hailey, moving to Alaska wasn't for certain. The cold was somewhat of a concern as well. It was one thing to gear up and put on the layers, but what would happen when I shifted? Would the cold air be too much for my Everglades coat and body? We certainly didn't need to bulk up for the winter around there.

As the night went on, I made sure to spend some time with each of my clanmates and friends; there was a slight chance that night would be a permanent farewell. As the night stretched on and I grew tired, I said my good-byes then found my sister.

"I need to head out," I told her. "My flight is

kinda early. Want to go for one last run through the 'Glades?"

She grinned and yanked off her shirt. In seconds, we'd both shifted and took off running through Everglades National Park. The lush greens surrounded me and I deeply inhaled the scent of the thick, tropical air. Bugs chirped, singing us along, and I ran close to the swampy lands to feel the damp, squishy mud under my feet. I jumped into the swamp and swam for a short time, dodging Hailey as she swam around me.

We splashed and played like we were kids again. Eventually, we got out, shook off our fur and continued the run to my apartment building.

"I'll be here bright and early to pick you up," Hailey said as she pulled me into a tight hug. "And I might just stow away with you."

"You'd be the best contraband ever." I kissed her cheek before going inside to shower.

3
COOPER

After I went through the boarding process and entered the main lobby of the cruise ship, I took a moment to look around and orient myself. The ship was massive, holding a few thousand staterooms and 14 decks. Fifteen hundred staff were onboard to run it all. And it was beautiful, too. I made my way to my room, pausing often to look at the map.

I finally found the stateroom, but didn't spend much time there. I rolled my suitcase in and noticed the space was far bigger than I'd expected; more like a decent-sized hotel room than the little cubby I'd envisioned a cruise ship stateroom as. Wanting to explore the other offerings of the ship, I headed right back out the door.

From the deck, I could see a vast landscape: on one side, ocean; on the other, mountain. In between was all forest, ice and snow. I checked out the pools and the other amenities, like the fitness center, bumper cars, roller-skating, a flight simulator, tons of restaurants, a casino, many bars, several gift shops, two theaters, an infirmary, and a full-service spa. The place was like a mini city in itself.

After I ate what was maybe the fanciest lunch I'd ever had, I wandered the ship again. Now that we were actually sailing, things had calmed some on the deck as people settled into their rooms for their first day on board. I leaned against the railing and took in the view of the ocean drifting out behind us.

It was beautiful. With everything so conveniently located on one ship, it made sense that some Rangers would choose to sail and work onboard—but most of them were not likely shifters. I needed to be able to run, and running along the top deck's jogging track wasn't exactly an option for me. Sure, as a human, I could put in the miles. But I obviously couldn't exactly take off, bounding around the ship as a bear. I'd have to restrict my shifting severely, and I most definitely couldn't do that long-term.

I loved the feeling of my feet on the cold ground, the icy air whipping through my fur, the majesty of being able to become a great animal at will, then change back to a highly intelligent species of my own volition. I'd never truly understand how shifters came to be—probably no more than humans understand how they came to be. But, origins or purpose aside, I loved being a shifter and everything about it. I considered it my greatest blessing to have been given such a rare gift. To stay on a ship all the time—even one so grand—would mean forfeiting that gift.

I checked my watch and decided it was time to get cleaned up. We didn't have a full day of instruction that day, more of a get-to-know-you introduction sort of thing, but I still wanted to be prepared. I showered and gathered my things, then headed to the room I'd been assigned to use as a classroom, arriving twenty minutes early. No one else had arrived yet, so I made sure things were in place and that I had everything I'd need. I wrote my name on the whiteboard on one wall and arranged the chairs to face me so that it was just like a classroom.

My group started to arrive, and as each one entered, I shook his or her hand and introduced myself. I also made sure to get in a good whiff of each student so I would know if any shifters were on board. As of then, in my group of eight, I could sense three: two wolves and an eagle. I'd have to be careful about my language. I never expected to have a group of all shifters, but it would have been nice to not have to edit as I spoke. I was used to being around shifters most of the time and realized I'd been a bit spoiled by it.

I waited until five minutes after the expected start time. I figured with a ship so big and everyone being new, someone might take an extra few minutes to find the room. When it seemed that everyone had arrived, I started with a simple exercise where we all went around and gave our names and why we were there. Breaking the ice. I knew they'd probably groan at it, but if we were going to be spending all week together, I thought it was best that they all be somewhat acquainted with each other.

When that was complete, I started telling them a bit about myself and my experience as a Ranger. A full twenty-five minutes after the designated start time, the door flung open and a woman rushed in, clearly frazzled. She slipped into the first seat she came to, dropped her things unceremoniously, and gave me a sympathetic grimace.

"I'm so, so sorry," she said. She hunched down,

trying to make herself smaller as everyone turned to look at her.

I stared at her for a moment in disbelief. *How could she be so late? But besides that, how could she be so gorgeous?* My breath caught when I looked at her. Someone that enchanting was going to be in my group for the week? I wasn't sure how I'd focus. If she'd sat in front of me, I would have been in trouble, so it would probably be best if she were in the back of the room.

It was rude, however, for her to have come in so late. Her good looks couldn't excuse her actions. Maybe she was used to that, but she wasn't going to get away with that there. I crossed my arms and gave her a displeased look.

"You missed introductions, so why don't you go ahead and stand up here and introduce yourself." I gestured to the space beside me at the front of the room.

Her face reddened, but she pushed herself up and came to stand beside me.

"Uh, I'm Alexis Hale. S...sorry I'm late..."

She looked at me questioningly.

"How about telling us where you're from and why you're here," I suggested.

"I'm from Florida. The Everglades. I'm here to check out the program and hopefully become an Alaskan Park Ranger onboard this and other cruise ships."

"Thank you."

As she walked past me to head to her seat, I got a taste of her scent. She was a bear shifter, and beyond that, smelled like lilac and vanilla. Beautiful *and* a shifter? I felt my member twitch in my pants, swallowed hard and faced the group.

She quickly took her seat and I resumed my instruction, and I was careful to avoid her eyes as I spoke. The one time I had, I lost my train of thought and had to clear my throat. I managed to make it through everything I wanted to cover that day. When I dismissed the class, I caught Alexis' gaze and motioned for her to come to the front.

She stood a few feet from me and hung her head slightly, making eye contact through her lashes. "I'm sorry I was late, I—"

"Please try to be on time tomorrow," I said. "Today was just introductions, but tomorrow, the real work starts."

"Yes...sir," she replied, sounding unsure of how to address me.

"Cooper is fine."

"Right." She pressed her lips together. "It won't happen again, I promise."

I nodded and watched her walk away. Already, things on the ship had become interesting.

4
ALEXIS

So far, my trip had been amazing. When Hailey dropped me off at the airport, I'd said my goodbyes and left Florida behind me for the week. I loved flying, and I immersed myself in the travel experience. I'd been to that airport before, of course, but not the one I had a layover in and not the one I landed at in Alaska. I took in as many details as I could and talked to people while waiting to board and then again on the plane.

By the time I actually saw the boat, I was so excited, I could hardly sit still. Once I was through check-in and on my own, that's when the real adventure began. I went to drop my bags off in my room first—I didn't want to be weighed down as I looked around—but even my room distracted me. I flopped down on the big bed and stretched out, flipping through the channels on the TV and seeing what options I had for room service and entertainment. I settled on the channel that showed how far we would sail.

After a few minutes of unpacking, I changed into my business casual attire and placed my traveling outfit in my dirty clothes bag. With my phone ready to take photos and my card key, I left the room. I snapped pics left and right and talked to everyone I stood by for more than a few seconds. Lunch was its own experience. I opted for the buffet that day, though I'd been told I could eat in the dining room for every meal. Once I saw the huge variety, there was no way I'd be satisfied with having just one entree and a few sides.

I walked through every section of the buffet, filling two plates with food, and as I sat to eat, I was joined by an older woman. She told me she was taking a vacation by herself for the first time after losing her husband. Her story was sad, but inspiring, nonetheless, and she assured me that I'd find love like that one day. I smiled as I forced myself to finish my food. I had taken too much, clearly, but I couldn't just waste it.

I nearly waddled back to my room with plans to change into my swimsuit and hop into the hot tub for a bit to digest. As I dug through my bag, I planned for the next day, hanging up the outfit I'd wear and then reached for my itinerary. I didn't want to be late on the first day. As I looked down the list, I saw that class started right after breakfast the next day at 10 a.m. Perfect.

Then my heart stopped. For that day, there was one little sentence that I'd completely missed. At 2 p.m., there was a scheduled meet and greet introduction session lasting two hours. My stomach sank as I checked the time: 2:18. I'd missed almost twenty minutes of it already and had no idea where it was.

I snatched up my purse and map and bolted from the room. I waited for the elevator while trying to find the right spot on the map.

A kind man standing beside me asked if I needed help finding my way. "I've been on this ship three times before," he said.

"Oh, thank you." I sighed in relief. "I need Meeting Room 2B."

He pulled his eyebrows together and looked over my shoulder. "Oh gosh. I'm afraid I don't know where that is."

My anxiety spiked. "No problem, thanks anyway."

When the elevator let me off on the correct deck, I rushed through the hall, scanning the walls for the room. The deck I was on must have been reserved for corporate events and staff rooms, judging by the look of it. I passed meeting rooms, a break room, and a few offices. Finally, I saw "Meeting Room 2B" on one of the doors.

I opened the door and slid into the first chair I could find. Of course, it was enough of a commotion to make the entire group turn to look at me. I gave an apologetic smile but felt horrible. *How could I let this happen? I will be known as the late girl for the rest of the week. I'm never the late girl!* A knot formed in my stomach and jumped to my throat when the instructor brought me up front to introduce myself.

My mind was scrambled and I blurted out my name. I figured the group had said more, but I had no idea what. I looked over at the instructor for guidance and my heart skipped when my eyes met his intense stare. I felt even more embarrassed as I muttered where I was from.

Once my moment of shame ended, I sat down and tried to be the best student I could be. I took notes, though there wasn't much to write down that day. The instructor, Cooper Hurst, talked about his own experiences as a Ranger in Glacier Bay and what it might be like for us to become Rangers one day.

I hoped I could sneak out without talking to anyone and make a fresher start the following day, but no luck. Cooper called me up to talk to him as the rest of the class left. Would this never be over? I wasted no time apologizing to him again. I wanted him to know that was not like me, but he interrupted me just to reprimand me again.

By the time I left the room, I felt like a complete idiot. So what if the instructor was hot? If he was going to make a point of repeatedly telling me not to be late, then maybe he was just an asshole like that; someone who loved to point out other people's flaws just to make himself feel better.

It wasn't quite dinner time yet, so I walked around the ship, trying to get enough of a signal to call or text Hailey. I'd been able to text her before the ship took off, but now it seemed I was too far. Several texts remained on my phone, all with failed delivery.

I sat down in a comfy chair and watched the ocean stream out behind the boat. Maybe training wasn't going to be what I'd thought. If the instructor was that tough and strict, I might not even make it through training. After a few minutes, I took a deep breath and steadied myself.

If Hailey were here, she would tell me I was being crazy. She would say, "Lex, you don't know the guy. Maybe he had a bad day, too. Maybe it's his first time teaching and *he's* nervous. Letting down one person—if that's even what happened—will not decide your future."

I nodded and said to myself, "You're right, as always, Hail."

I couldn't let that one little mistake define my whole week. I'd messed up. Okay, fine. Who didn't? Time to let it go and enjoy my stay there. If nothing else, it was my vacation time.

That night, I opted to have dinner in the dining room, and as soon as I walked in the room, I knew it was the right choice. The sparkling chandeliers and beautiful decor lifted my spirits. I was happy to find that my waiter would be with me all week. He was nice and we chatted as he brought me my drink and meal. I felt much better, hadn't over eaten by too much, and knew it was time to get a bit of exercise in.

I stopped by my room to get my sweater and scarf. Inside the ship, the temperature was perfect, but on the outside decks, things were much chillier. I walked along the railing for a while, staring out at the vast amount of water around us. I couldn't see much of Alaska from there, but what I could see were distant mountains. My breath made white clouds and I pulled my scarf more tightly around me.

When I looked up, I was shocked to see so many stars. Down in the Everglades, we had plenty in the park. People always commented that they could see so many more than in Miami. But Alaska was another story. Billions of shimmering stars twinkled and a greenish hue smeared across the sky on one end. I gasped when I realized I was seeing the aurora borealis.

"Have you ever seen the Northern Lights before?"

The sudden voice startled me. I'd been so engrossed in the sky that I hadn't noticed someone coming up beside me. I looked over my shoulder and my face was instantly red.

"You said you were from Florida?" Cooper asked.

I nodded. "It's much warmer there." *What a thing to say. I should just run now before I make a bigger fool of myself.*

He chuckled. "I bet. There aren't too many places colder than Alaska in the States."

"Are you from here?"

"Born and raised. But I never get sick of that sight." He pointed to the green streaks in the sky. "It's amazing how it changes throughout the year. So many colors."

"It's really beautiful." I dared a look at him and found him returning the gesture. I gulped. "I just want you to know that I'm not a late person. Today was…"

He chuckled again. "No problem. It happens to all of us. I got there twenty minutes early to make sure I wasn't late myself."

"That's the sort of thing I normally do. Somehow, I missed the fact that we even had a session today. Between lunch and the ship, I was distracted."

"First time on a cruise?"

"Yeah. Won't be my last, though."

"I guess not if you'll be working on board."

"Right. I mean, even as a vacation. I'm not set on Alaska quite yet. This week is a way for me to check everything out and decide if I want to take the job."

He nodded. "You're quite far from home. I'd imagine it would be difficult to leave your family and clan. You must miss them."

When he said 'clan,' I pulled my eyebrows together. I hadn't noticed he was a shifter. I pointed my nose his way and drew in a deep breath to catch his scent. Sure enough, under his amazing-smelling cologne, I got a whiff of shifter—and bear, at that.

I laughed and shook my head. "Truth be told, I've been so busy here, I hadn't even noticed." I *had* noticed how incredibly hot he was, though. And the fact that he wasn't wearing a wedding ring.

"I'm told my scent isn't the strongest." He shrugged. "I would have thought that as an Alpha it would be amplified, but I guess it doesn't work that way."

"I guess not. Alpha, huh?" *Good looking and a leader? How the hell was he still single?*

"My clan isn't too far from where we sailed off from."

"Guess that explains things."

He gave me a questioning look. "Oh yeah? What things?"

"Just your...strong leadership style."

He put his hand to his face. "I'm not mean, I promise. I..."

I looked at him, waiting.

"If I can be perfectly honest," he said with an unsure expression, "the only reason I talked to you after class was because I wanted an *excuse* to talk to you."

I swallowed hard as my heart skipped. "You could have just said, 'Hi.'"

"I may be good at talking to a group of people, but I'm not always great one-on-one—obviously, or I wouldn't be telling you all about my flaws in our first real conversation."

I let my smile spread to take up my whole face. "I like that. Saves me having to find out later when it's already too late."

"Too late?"

"Have you ever really liked someone, then found out something awful about them, but it was too late, so you just stuck it out since you had strong feelings? But then it turned out to be a disaster anyhow and you wish you would have just listened to your sister and avoided the whole thing, but—" I realized I was rambling and stopped short. "You know?"

"I think I know what you mean. Sorry that happened to you."

I lifted a shoulder. "It's over now. But my point was, I think it's nice to get the flaws out in the open right from the start. No surprises."

"Then, I guess it's your turn." He gave me a mischievous smile.

"Oh, right..." *Nice plan, Alexis. Now you've got your-*

self stuck. "Well, I get easily distracted. I'm too 'excitable,' my mother always says. I can't help it, though. When I find something interesting, I pay attention to it." I shrugged. "I guess it can make me a little…scatterbrained at times? So, I do a lot of planning to make up for that. I keep lists and schedules and rely on them. It usually works. Except for today."

"That's acceptable."

I laughed. "Good. Now that that's out of the way…"

"Maybe we should discuss our good points, too?" He raised an eyebrow. "Like that you're very friendly and outgoing, energetic and amazed at the world. I admire that."

I felt my face flush and looked down. "Your good points are obvious. Super hot, leader, knowledgeable, experienced, funny, kind. Punctual."

He laughed. "My mother would be thrilled to hear you call me punctual. I guess all her yelling finally sunk in." Then he gave me an amused look. "Super hot?"

I bit my lip. "Don't act like you don't think it's true."

"I'm just glad *you* think it's true. I guess that's something we have in common then."

My stomach jumped. "Yeah? And the punctual thing, too. I swear."

He laughed again. I loved that sound.

"I'll prove it," I insisted. "Tomorrow. Definitely. I'll be the first one there."

"I'll have to make sure I'm extra early then." He held my gaze as he gave me a heart-stopping smile. "See you tomorrow."

"Bright and early."

I barely slept that night. My heart was so full and my mind was tumbling. Cooper. There was something special about him. Not just his good looks. I liked him. Genuinely liked him. It was the first time I'd even let myself feel anything after the disaster with my ex. It was a little scary, to be out there again, hoping and dreaming, feeling those butterflies in my stomach. But it felt so good at the same time. We had all week. Who knew what would come of it.

5
ALEXIS

When I got up in the morning, I looked over the outfit I'd planned for the day. It was definitely professional, but not the cutest thing ever. I pulled out all of my clothes for the week, took a few minutes to rearrange things, and felt satisfied that I'd made each outfit a bit cuter. I dressed and put my hair up into a high ponytail, swiped a few coats of mascara over my lashes and accessorized. I stood in front of the mirror feeling good about how I looked; I hoped Cooper would feel the same.

After checking myself over one last time, I headed out the door. I was early that day—very early. Partly because I wanted to prove I wasn't the 'late girl,' but more so, I wanted a few minutes with

Cooper before the others arrived. When I got to the classroom, no one was there yet, but I was more than twenty minutes early. I went inside and turned on the lights, choosing a seat closer to the front. Not in the first row, where I wanted to be, but one row back so it wasn't so obvious I was crushing on the instructor.

Cooper entered just a few minutes later. "Ahh, glad to see you here on time today, Miss Hale," he said in a mock stern voice.

"Well, you know, the instructor is very strict, so I had to make sure I made a good impression on the first full day."

His mouth fell into a half smile. "I'd say you accomplished that."

My throat went dry and I took a moment to look him over. His polo shirt was close fitting, hinting at his muscular chest. His thick biceps were visible past the edge of his sleeve—and made me wonder about the parts that *weren't* visible. My face warmed and I changed my line of thinking. If I started picturing him naked now, I'd never be able to concentrate.

Other members of the group filed in moments later. For the time being, I'd been saved from my impure thoughts. But our time alone had also been cut very short. As he began teaching, we kept catching each other's eye. I smiled freely. His smiles were more subtle and stifled. I suspected he didn't want to be instructing with a huge grin on his face. It was fun, though, and I got a little thrill each time our eyes met.

When we broke for lunch, my heart raced in anticipation. Would he ask me to join him? Was that even okay? Should I ask him to join me? I didn't want to come off clingy, though; I knew Hailey would yell at me for that. She was a big fan of playing hard to get.

I went on my way with the rest of the group, chatting with them as we walked, though I was vividly aware that Cooper was several people ahead of me. As we all went off to get food, the group scattered a bit. I lost sight of Cooper in line, but now that I looked for a seat, I saw him sitting a table. Alone.

When our eyes met, he gestured to the seat next to his, motioning for me to join him. I hurried over and set my plate down.

"It's like high school lunch all over again," he said, chuckling. "Are you sure it's acceptable to sit with the teacher?"

"I don't care what the others think. I don't mind being called teacher's pet." I winked at him.

He opened his mouth to reply just as another classmate walked over.

"Mind if I join you?"

It was Henry, a nice guy from somewhere in the middle of the country. Not a shifter, but friendly. *He'd make a great Ranger*, I thought.

"Of course." Cooper forced a smile, but when he looked at me, I could see slight disappointment behind it.

I pressed my lips together in a similar, brief, disappointed smile, then turned toward Henry and started making conversation that all three of us could participate in. By the end, I'd learned a lot more about Montana and Henry, but not Cooper. The fact that he'd been visibly disappointed, however, made up for it.

At the end of the class day, I stalled, taking my time to gather my things. My plan worked. The room cleared and it was just Cooper and me.

He walked over and perched on the edge of the desk next to mine. "I'm sorry we didn't get to talk more at lunch. I thought maybe we could have dinner together?"

His words brought a huge grin to my face and I nodded. I didn't trust myself to speak without saying something stupid.

"Great." He glanced at his watch. "Meet me by the elevators at 6? Is that a good time?"

"Sure. See you then."

I nearly skipped back to my room, then stared at my clothes, wondering if there was a decent dress shop on board.

6

COOPER

I hadn't been able to get a cell signal since we'd left the port, but as an instructor, I had access to the staff phones that were powered by satellite. I walked to the staff break room and took a seat, then dialed Kylie, my sister. What Alexis had said before about sisters giving romantic advice was just as true for my sister and I. But what I hadn't admitted to Alexis was that I always listened to my sister.

It was good to hear her voice when she answered. "Hey there, little sis."

"Oh good. I hoped it would be you and not some damn telemarketer. I hate when I have to answer an unknown number. Anyhow, how's it going?"

"Great. My group is very...interesting."

"Interesting? How so?"

"More diverse than I expected. People from all over. About half are shifters of various species, all ages, men and…women…"

"Oh yeah?" She chuckled. "And women?"

She knew me too well. I couldn't hide a thing from her. "Yes, women. I…may have met someone?"

"What? You've been there less than two days! Tell me everything!"

I recounted the way Alexis had stumbled into my life, our encounter the night before and our time together at lunch.

"Okay, and what do you plan to do about it?" she asked when I told her I was disappointed that our lunch had been interrupted.

"I asked her out. We're having dinner in about an hour."

"Nice move, bro. I do expect full details, of course."

"Of course."

I agonized over my outfit. That was the sort of thing I always relied on Kylie for help with, but without her there to tell me if what I wore looked decent, I'd have to just take the chance.

When I walked to the group of elevators, I found Alexis already waiting.

"You know," I said as I put my arm in front of the doors to keep them from closing on her, "You don't have to keep proving to me that you're not the late sort."

She smiled at me. "I'm usually early. It's the only way I can make sure I'm not late."

We sat for dinner and I was amazed at how she talked to the waiter like she'd known him forever. Apparently, she'd had the same guy the night before and they'd struck up some conversation. It seemed that no matter who she was around, Alexis found someone to chat with and had a good time doing it.

"I have to ask," I said while we waited for our meal. "What made you choose Alaska? It's so far and so different from Florida."

"A few reasons. I want to experience the world and live in a bunch of different places. This job opportunity was so perfect, I had to at least come check it out. And I thought it might not be bad to get out of Florida for a while."

"Does that have anything to do with the advice from your sister that you didn't take?"

She blew out a sigh. "Yes. My ex-boyfriend is there and things didn't...end well."

"His loss."

She gave a half smile. "My dodged bullet."

"That bad, huh?"

"Well, I figured if the guy cheated on me before we even got to the more serious stages of our relationship, I'd probably be setting myself up for a lifetime of heartbreak if I stayed with him."

"I don't blame you. There are few things more hurtful than cheating."

"Yeah. But Hailey was right. When I found out he'd cheated on his last girlfriend, she told me to watch out; that if he'd done it before, he'd probably do it again. I thought it would be different with me for some reason. How stupid." She shook her head.

"I can't imagine anyone looking at you, then choosing to be with someone else. *That* was stupid."

"Thanks." She looked down and a blush crept over her cheeks. "You've never cheated on anyone?"

"Was never even tempted to. Once I make a commitment to something or someone, I follow it through. Maybe to a fault, even; I don't know."

"To a fault? How is that possible?"

Now it was my turn to blow out a sigh. "My ex. It was clear the relationship wasn't really going anywhere. We'd been together for a few years. I thought about proposing, but mostly because it was the next logical step. We both wanted to have kids some day and we seemed to get along fine, so I thought we'd have a simple life together. But Kylie, my sister, knew better. She said there was no passion. The love wasn't deep enough. When I told her I figured I'd propose, she stopped me. She asked if I was truly happy, and when I said I wasn't *un*happy, she basically told me I was settling and it would be a mistake. I took some time to really think about it, and she was right. We'd been together so long, we just...stayed together. There was nothing really wrong in our relationship, we just didn't have the passion."

"Well, there's no point in being with someone without that."

I picked up my glass, eager to move on with the conversation. "Here's to smarter choices and new horizons, with just the right amount of passion and commitment."

She tapped her glass to mine. "Here's to finding true love."

"You said you want to see the world. Where else have you been?"

"Not many places yet, actually. I planned to go away for school, but the best program was right there in Florida. Alaska is really my first big trip."

"Well, I don't want to lure you away too shamelessly, but it's beautiful here. And huge. You could take years just exploring Alaska."

"What I've seen so far has been so...enchanting. I'm looking forward to seeing more, though I wish we could get off the boat to really see it."

"I guess you'll just have to accept the job and move here, then." I shrugged.

She laughed. "I guess so."

"And you know, there are a lot more men here than women. If you want to work on that whole finding true love thing, you'd certainly have your pick."

"Ahh, I'm not too sure about that."

I raised an eyebrow at her.

"I may have already found what I'm looking for."

My throat felt parched as I held her gaze. The burning in my heart, the flutter in my stomach; that was the passion Kylie wanted for me. That excitement at being together, that newness of learning about each other, that feral desire to touch one another. I got hard just thinking about being closer to her. The cold shower I'd taken the night before hadn't stopped my vivid dreams. We had such little time together, just a handful of days. But still, that seemed too soon to be sleeping together. I swallowed hard again. She drove me so crazy, I didn't know if I'd be able to be a gentleman around her.

By the time we were through dinner and dessert, I noticed that the dining room had emptied some. When I glanced at my watch, I saw that we'd been there for almost two hours. The cruise staff hadn't said anything, but I figured they probably wanted their table.

"Care to walk under the stars for a bit?" I offered.

"I'd love to."

We left the restaurant and I took her hand. That little gesture alone made my heart race. Her hand was warm and soft and I slowly inhaled the scent of her, committing it to memory.

We walked along the upper deck, pausing to gaze at the stars now and then. When we got to the back of the ship, the sky was on fire with brilliant red and orange streaks of the aurora borealis—almost like a sign just for us, echoing that our hearts burned for one another. We stopped to watch it for a while. But it became too much for me.

I slipped my arm around her, and when she turned her head to look over at me, I leaned in and pressed my lips to hers. She turned to fully face me, her whole body pressing against mine in an embrace as our mouths moved together. I didn't want to ever stop, but I had to.

I broke the kiss and ran my thumb across her cheek. *My sister was right. Having the passion is absolutely necessary.*

7

COOPER

It was getting harder and harder to concentrate. After our first dinner together, Alexis and I had gone out every night. We kissed, but that was as far as it went. I could barely hold out any longer, thinking I might explode every time she smiled at me. I was falling hard and fast and I never wanted that feeling to end. Only problem was, we had two days left on the ship before she'd be going back to Florida. If she took the job and returned to Alaska, it wouldn't be for more than a month, when the prime cruising season started at the end of May.

I didn't know what I was going to do then. How could I say goodbye to her? I planned to make that night extra special. We would be out of the classroom a lot that day, which was good. I could distract myself more easily than it would be to try and avoid looking over at her constantly. Out on the deck, where I could point out landmarks and teach the group how to show others the sights, I could focus better.

After class, she waited as she had every day. When everyone else was gone, I walked over and stole a quick kiss.

"I was thinking that maybe we should do things a little different tonight," I said.

"Buffet instead of dining room?"

I laughed. "We could... Or..." I took her hand and walked her out of the room.

"Where are we going?"

"I want to show you our other option for the evening."

I led her out to the outside deck of the ship and pointed to a small boat sailing toward the coast. We were close to Kodiak Island, then would have the following day at sea as we headed back to Glacier Bay. Though the rest of the ship would only have a view of the island from the decks, I found out that staff could take a tender boat and go to the nearby coast.

"You said you wanted to get off the boat and

explore. I thought I'd give you an exclusive tour of the island."

She bit her lip and grinned at me. "Really? I would love that!"

We ate dinner on the ship, then headed down to catch the tender. I had a sack of things ready for us as we made our way down onto the smaller vessel. Once we had docked, I lead her to a more secluded area.

"I thought it would be nice to shift and go for a run."

Her mouth popped open slightly and she looked around. "Yeah..."

I laughed. "I'll turn away, of course."

Her face went pink and she smiled. "What if I don't?"

I winked and gave her a mischievous smile. "You're free to check out the goods if you'd like."

I turned my back to her and pulled off my shirt. Then, I bent to take off my pants and boxers, placing everything in the sack before shifting. I faced away from her and heard her shift, then turned back.

The only bad part was that we wouldn't be able to talk for a while. We might have both been bears, but we weren't in the same clan, so we didn't have the benefit of the mental clan link that allowed us to communicate with our clanmates while in our ursine forms.

She had no trouble keeping up, though, and she was able to communicate in her own way. When she wanted to pause to sniff at a plant more, she made a little growl and put her paw on mine for a moment. I watched her explore with her nose, waiting until she was ready to move on. When she'd had enough, she came back to me and rubbed her head against my middle.

It made the fur on my neck stand up at attention, and I took off running to distract myself. When we got to the place I wanted to show her, I wasn't sure how to go about telling her I was going to shift back. I didn't want to be suddenly naked in front of her. Why hadn't I considered how awkward it might be? Just as I was trying to figure out what to do, she nudged the sack with her nose, then sat beside it.

I nodded and went behind the biggest bush I could find to shift back. "Want to toss that to me?"

She took the sack's strap in her teeth and whipped her head to send the sack flying my way. I dressed and left the bag there for her, minus the blanket I'd brought along. She followed my lead and shifted back as well.

"That was a beautiful run," she said. "Is this what it's like where you live?"

"Not too different. A bit more ice here, maybe."

She looked around appreciatively. "I could see living here. I really could. It's absolutely stunning."

I didn't want to get my hopes up too high, but I desperately wanted her to stay. I took her hand and pulled her closer to me, wrapping my arms around her.

"You have to do what's best for you," I whispered to her. "But know that if you choose to move to Alaska, I'll be here."

She rested her head on my shoulder. "That's reason enough for me."

I spread the blanket out and we lay back, looking up at the stars. From here, our view of the sky was edged with tree tops, but it didn't get in the way of the incredible view. My only problem was, the view was much more interesting right beside me.

I rolled to my side to kiss her, and once we started, I knew we weren't going to stop. We were already lying down. If I'd planned it, that would have been the perfect move. I hadn't, but now I was very glad I'd thought to bring the blanket. Our make out session heated up in no time, and before I knew it, she rolled on top of me.

There was no hiding my erection now. She pressed her hips into my hardness, rubbing herself against me. If she didn't want to sleep with me, then I'd misread all the signs.

I let my hands roam under her shirt. Since she was lying on me, I couldn't reach her breasts, so I dragged my fingers along her spine. She ran her hands under my shirt as well, almost tickling me as she stroked my sides.

I needed to be able to touch her more, so I rolled us over so that I could caress her breasts. She hadn't put her bra back on after shifting, I'd noticed. Was that just for convenience since we'd have to shift back? Or maybe she wanted this as much as I did. I sure hoped so.

She let out a small moan when I pinched her nipple. I reached my hand down to her knee and slowly slid my hand up until it brushed the edge of her skirt. I slid underneath, waiting for her to stop me, and when she didn't, I let my hand graze over her. I sucked in a breath when I realized that she hadn't put her panties back on, either.

She moaned and pressed into me. When I dared to slip my finger between her folds, she was already wet. My dick throbbed in my pants, begging to be let free. Not yet, though.

I slipped my finger inside her and she started rocking her hips with the motion, nibbling gently on my neck, sending shivers through me.

"Are you sure about this?" I breathed into her ear.

"Definitely." She pushed her hips up in confirmation.

"We haven't known each other very long..." What was I doing? Trying to talk her out of it? *Stupid.*

"No, but this is our...fourth, maybe sixth date?"

I didn't know which things counted. Our dinners together for sure. Did our lunches, count, too? Either way, we'd spent the majority of the last four days together. I guess that did sort of compress many months of a relationship into a short time.

"What's wrong?" she asked. She rubbed the spot between my eyes, where my brow furrowed when I thought too hard. "If you don't want to..."

I laughed once. "It's definitely not that. I just don't want you to regret it later and for me to feel like I coerced you into it or something."

She reached down to my pants and pulled on the waist until the button popped open. Then she forced the zipper down and pulled my pants down just enough to let my cock spring free. She reached for it hungrily and stroked it several times, her hand smooth and warm in contrast to the frigid air as she moved it up and down my shaft.

I closed my eyes, trying hard not to finish too soon. Yanking my shirt over my head, I attempted to cool down, but then she positioned me at her opening.

"Wait." I pulled back a little and focused on my breathing. She was too hot. Too perfect. And I wanted her too goddamn badly.

She rubbed along my back, waiting. After a few moments, she sat up and pulled her dress over her head, standing before me completely naked. As I took in the glorious sight of her curves in the moonlight, she began to slowly sway her hips. I sat with my pants open and cock at full mast as she bent to tease me, pressing her breasts against my face. Swiveling her hips to the unheard music, she licked her lips before tugging my pants down and off.

I straightened out my legs and reached up for her hips, pulling her down onto my lap. She lifted herself enough so she could get into position and slid down on me slowly, letting me sink fully inside her as we both let out deep moans of pleasure.

She rocked back and forth on my lap, her arms wrapped tightly around me. I held her hips and moved with her, raising her up slightly so she could slam back down onto me.

We sped up, but I needed to get into a better position, so I wrapped my arms around her and leaned her back so I was on top of her. From there, I could thrust into her more effectively and get a better view of her.

I caressed her breasts with my mouth and dragged my tongue along her neck. She grabbed my ass and as she pulled me in deeper, I sped up more, feeling myself growing close again. I wasn't sure if she was close or not, so I slowed down and made circular motions with my hips, pounding into her as I moved. She dug her nails into my back and moaned, and with each thrust, she cried out, slamming her hips into me in response.

She wrapped her legs around my waist, flexing them tightly to deepen the thrusts. I sped up again, but this time, when I got close, I didn't hold back, pounding her hard and fast until I released everything inside her.

She cried out, shuddering around me as she bucked her hips involuntarily. As she opened her eyes, she let out a satisfied sigh. "I feel like I've been waiting for that for months."

I laughed and rested my forehead against hers. "I feel like I'm going to want to do that for months."

"Mmm. Me, too." She smiled and kissed me as she ran her fingers through my sweat-drenched hair. "It's not so cold here after all."

As I looked down at her naked body, though, I saw her skin in gooseflesh. Living in Florida probably meant that even this more mild Alaskan weather was too cold for her.

"Sorry. I forget you're a warm weather woman." I wrapped the blanket up and over her.

She snuggled into it. "Just means you'll have to stay close. And naked. Better body heat transference that way."

"Survival 101," I added.

"Exactly. And I'm pretty sure your naked body next to mine would help me survive anything."

I curled up behind her, enjoying the feeling of her body and warmth against me.

8
ALEXIS

Once we got closer to land, my texts to Hailey were finally able to go through. I didn't want to wait for a text back, so I called her; when she answered, I unleashed a torrent of excitement upon her.

"Wow, he sounds amazing," she said when I'd gone through all of the Cooper details. "I can't believe none of your texts went through!"

"Yeah, there isn't much service at sea. This was my first real chance."

"Are you still coming home?"

"What do you mean?"

"Well, now that you know you'll take the job, I didn't know if you'd stay there and start right away or extend your vacation a little to find a place."

"Oh." I pondered that for a moment. "No, that's silly. Of course I'll be home. I mean, it's not for sure yet."

"Oh." She sounded genuinely surprised. "I just thought with your excitement over Cooper, there was no way you wouldn't take it. Do you think a long-distance relationship will work?"

"I hadn't really thought about it. We haven't talked about it, either. I think we both just wanted to enjoy the time we do have without thinking about saying goodbye."

"Well, that's good. You shouldn't make such a huge life decision based on someone you've only known for a few days, even if it is getting serious already."

"It's not really serious. We've been out a bunch of times, but we haven't made commitments or anything."

"True, but you did already sleep with him. This isn't just a one-night stand. There are feelings involved."

I sighed. "There are. I might be falling in love."

"Slow it down, there, Lex. Don't do this to yourself. Take your time."

"I already asked him if he ever cheated. He never even considered it."

"Good, I'm glad to hear that. And hopefully, it's true. But Lex, cheating isn't the only reason not to be with someone. I'd hate to see you get so excited, move and then have things not work out."

"I know. But remember, Alaska was a real possibility even before Cooper. He just adds a little…"

"Incentive?"

"More like sweetness. He's the cherry on top, making it a perfect picture."

"Maybe he can come here to get you when you move so we can all meet him."

And she accused *me* of moving too fast? "I'm sure if that's what happens, he'll come visit."

"You didn't tell him you love him, did you?"

"No." But in truth, I'd thought about it. "Not yet."

"Just don't. Not until after you get home and see what becomes of this, okay?"

"Fine." I rolled my eyes, but I knew she was right. What if we had the fantasy scenario going on, where everything was paradise while on the ship, but once we got off and went back to the real world, things fell apart?

I still had nothing but thoughts of Cooper and our time together as I fell asleep that night. I was sad that we had just one full day left. Our last day of teaching would be short, then we'd have one last night together.

In the morning, I picked up my room in case we ended up there that night. We'd have to make the most of our last night together. The next morning, we'd all leave the ship and I'd take a plane home. My throat burned at the thought of it, but at least we had one more day.

∽

THE FOLLOWING MORNING, I bounced into the classroom, barely able to wait to see Cooper. We'd been arriving earlier and earlier to class to steal a few moments together, so I got there almost a half hour before the start time. He wasn't there, and as I sat, the time kept ticking by, my disappointment rising with each passing minute.

When the rest of the group started arriving, I was bummed that we missed our moment. *What could be holding him up?* I wondered. Then, a woman I hadn't seen before entered the room and marched to the front.

"Hello, all. I'm Becca Howard. I know this is your last day and that you've been working with Cooper Hurst. I'm afraid he's had an emergency and had to leave the ship late last night. I'll be filling in for today."

My heart stopped. Emergency? Left? He was gone? Off the ship?

"Is he coming back?" I blurted.

She gave me a flat look. "No."

"What was the emergency? Is he okay?" My mind whirled with possibilities.

"He's fine. Now, let's get on with the instruction and we'll finish up quickly so that you can enjoy the rest of your stay onboard."

I blinked through tears as my heart burned. We wouldn't have our last day—or night—together after all. I'd been so counting on those last moments, needing them. And now everything was cut short. He was gone. No goodbye, no final kiss. Nothing. As the class went on, I thought about calling him afterward to make sure he was okay. Gasping aloud, my blood turned to ice as I then realized the flaw in my plan: I never gave him my number and he never gave me his. I had no way to contact him.

"Everything okay?" Becca eyed me, stopping her explanation to address me.

"Yes, sorry."

But my mind spun. How would I contact him? I could try looking online, but what if I couldn't find him? The panic rose in my chest and didn't let up until class had ended.

While everyone else said their goodbyes and good lucks, I went to Becca with a piece of paper in my hand.

"Hi, Becca," I said. "I was wondering if you had a way to contact Cooper?"

"I can answer anything you need to know."

"Thank you, but I wanted to talk to him personally. We struck up a sort of...friendship this week and didn't get to say goodbye or exchange numbers."

Her eyes narrowed. "Friendship?"

My face grew hot and I nodded. "So, I really want to be able to talk to him again."

"I'm sorry. I don't have his number or anything."

"What about the cruise company? Would they have it?"

Her face was cold and hard. "They don't give out personal information on their visitors."

"Do you know him? Cooper? Could you get a message to him or can someone give him my number?"

"You want him to call you?"

"Very much so."

She gave a kind of sarcastic laugh. "I'm guessing you're not from here."

"No…"

"Well, let me save you some heartache. You don't want Cooper Hurst to call you."

"What do you mean?"

"Let's just say he has…quite the reputation." She gave a smug smile.

"Okay…? Well, are you able to get my number to him, then?"

"I'll give it to him, sure. But I wouldn't expect him to call. He never calls. He's just your average player."

"Cooper Hurst? He doesn't seem like the type."

She laughed. "They never do. Trust me, he does this sort of thing all the time." She gestured to me. "Finds a cute girl to hook up with, then he's gone, just like that. I hope you were smart enough not to sleep with him."

I swallowed hard and didn't say anything. It wasn't her business, anyway.

"Well, if you did, just be glad the whole thing is over. He's gotten what he wants from you, now the vacation is over, and you can go about your life doing whatever it was you had planned."

I gave her the paper I'd prepared. "If you could just make sure he gets this, please."

I hurried from the room, my throat tight. Back in

my room, I sobbed as I packed. I wandered through the ship, but couldn't eat dinner; I felt so lonely and just plain heartbroken.

Was anything Becca said true? Cooper didn't seem like that at all, but she was right: they never do seem like the type. My ex hadn't seemed like the cheating type, either, but he was. And did it even matter? If I had no way to contact Cooper, was it just over? Would he ever try to find me? Or was I just a fling?

That night, I had thought about telling him I was falling for him; that I wanted to continue our relationship. I had thought about taking the job in Alaska to be near him, but I didn't know what to do now. I didn't know if I'd ever see him again or hear from him. And if what Becca said was true, then he might have already forgotten about me. Completely devastated, I cried myself to sleep.

9

COOPER

The car wouldn't go fast enough for me. I leaned forward from the backseat and talked to the cab driver again.

"I'm sorry. I know you're going above the speed limit already, but there's been an emergency and I really need to get to the hospital fast. I'll pay more if you can drive a little faster."

He sped up, but it didn't stop my worry. The late-night call had been the worst of my life. Someone had come to my room to wake me. It was so late, I'd already been asleep, dreaming peacefully of Alexis after our perfect night together. A staff member said there was an emergency call for me.

That walk to the staffroom seemed to take forever. I had no other information, but assumed it must have been something with my clan or my family. When I picked up the receiver, my mother was on the other end.

"Oh, thank God, Cooper. It's Kylie. She's been in a car accident."

"What? Is she okay?"

"They're flying her to Bartlett Regional. Is there any way you can come?"

"Come? To the hospital? Is it serious?"

"Cooper..." There was a long silence and I heard her stifle a sob. "They're saying they don't know if she's going to make it."

"I'll be there as soon as I possibly can."

I'd hung up and went into overdrive. I hunted down the person in charge of the Ranger instruction program and told him what had happened. Rushing back to my room, I threw my things in my bag and hurried back out. Only after the door closed behind me, my room keys inside for check out, did I stop to think I should have written Alexis a note and slipped it under her door.

Well, I'd have to somehow get her number later and explain everything. As I hurried down to where I'd catch the tender, I thought of Alexis. We'd miss our last night together. I wouldn't get to say goodbye. If she didn't come back, I'd never see her again. The thought was unreal, just like the fact that my sister might have been dying at that very moment. No, neither of those things would be true. I wouldn't let them be.

As I waited for ages for the boat, I used the two women against each other. When thoughts about Kylie became too suffocating, I thought about Alexis. When thoughts about Alexis became too heartbreaking, I thought about Kylie. My heart lurched and my stomach ached. I wanted Alexis there with me. I wanted to have her hold my hand and rub my back, telling me it was going to be okay; to wait there with me and make things not seem quite so terrible.

In an irrational moment, I had thought of rushing up to her room and waking her, either to say goodbye or to beg her to come with me. But the boat had shown up then and I couldn't take the time to wait for the next. I'd contact Alexis just as soon as I could manage.

Watching the streets fly by all too slowly, I was too close to be distracted any longer. All I could think about was my sister and family. We couldn't lose Kylie. We just couldn't.

The cab finally pulled up to the hospital and I jumped out, almost forgetting to pay, then almost forgetting to grab my bag. I hurried to the floor my mom had mentioned and found the ICU. My mom was sitting outside the room, staring blankly at the TV in the waiting area. When she looked over and saw me coming, she jumped to her feet.

"You're here." She pulled me into a tight hug and squeezed for a long time. "Your clan is here. Most of them."

I walked around the corner to see several members of my clan, waved to them and assured them I'd return soon. First, I got more details from my mom about what had happened and what the doctors were saying before I went in to see Kylie. My dad was there, holding her hand.

She was hooked up to many tubes and machines, sleeping, which I guess was best. Covered in bandages, she didn't even look like herself. I sat for a moment, terrified, holding her other hand, then talked quietly with my dad for a time.

When I finally went back out to the waiting room, Jace was the first person who came to me.

"Hey man, we're here. Whatever you need, you let us know."

I put my hand on his shoulder to steady myself for a moment. As my oldest and best friend, he'd been with me through many things. I could always count on Jace to help me out.

"Thanks. I can't even think straight right now."

We sat and I talked with my other clanmates. Luckily, Carson and Max hadn't killed each other while I was gone. They'd done a fine job in my absence, Jace assured me.

As the hours grew late and members of the waiting party shrank, Jace remained with me. He was almost part of the family, almost another brother to Kylie, so he wasn't going anywhere any time soon.

"You want to know something crazy?" I said to him as we sat alone in the waiting room.

"What's that?" he asked through a yawn.

"I may have found the love of my life."

"What's this now?" He sat up to listen better.

I told him about Alexis and our time together. "But I rushed off the boat so fast to be here, I didn't have time to leave my number. I feel terrible that I couldn't say goodbye, and I don't know if she's coming back to Alaska. I may have lost her."

"If it's meant to be, it will be. Maybe you can get her number from the cruise company somehow."

"Yeah, I planned to try tomorrow. As soon as I have the chance."

"She won't get away. No way. After the disaster with Becca, you're due for a good woman."

"Becca wasn't a bad woman."

He raised an eyebrow at me. "No, okay. I guess while you were together, she wasn't. But after you broke up with her?"

I sighed. "Yeah. *That* part was a disaster."

The way our relationship had fizzled out, I hadn't expected Becca to be too upset when I told her that I just wasn't in love with her anymore. I thought she'd been feeling the same way, that she'd lost feelings for me over the years, too. But when I ended it, she had gotten very angry. She told me she'd been planning our future and dreaming of our wedding and that she'd wasted years on me.

She hadn't said, though, that she loved me as much she didn't want to lose me. I suspected she just wanted to be married and have kids and didn't care much who the husband was; like I was just a pawn in her master plan. Luckily, she had found another man fairly quickly. Once she started dating, and more specifically once she beat me to dating again, she chilled out. Now, she didn't glare at me the whole time a clan meeting was going on. She stopped talking to me for the most part, but I was okay with that.

"Alexis has been hurt, too," I said. "I don't think she's as set on her perfect picture as Becca was. Not that she doesn't have tons of plans. But she's up for adventure, wants to see the world, all of that."

"What if she doesn't want to settle down at all?" Jace asked. "What if it's Becca Syndrome in reverse?"

I ran my fingers through my hair. Was I missing it again? Were my feelings for Alexis stronger than hers for me? "I don't know. Maybe she won't. I'm going to be careful this time. And I'm going to be open from the start. No more hiding my feelings, thinking they might change or come back or whatever. With Becca, I kept thinking that if we just went ahead and got married, the love and passion would return."

"I don't think it works like that."

"Apparently not." I twisted my fingers together. "I wish she were here, though—Alexis, that is. You'll love her. If she were here, she would have struck up a conversation with every nurse and doctor on the floor, entertaining the clan while they waited with us. She'd keep my mind off this horrible reality."

Jace put his hand on my shoulder. "Kylie is going to come through this. I know it. She has to. She's too strong and stubborn to go out in something as generic as a car accident. Think about how mad she'd be if she knew everyone was here, seeing her looking so crappy."

I shook my head with wide eyes. "Oh no. We'll never tell her that. It's been just me, our parents and you. If she knows about anyone else, she'll flip."

We laughed, and it felt good to let go a bit.

I waited until a decent hour and called the staff on the cruise ship. They were all busy, getting ready for departure, but after giving them some fake law enforcement credentials, someone finally gave me Alexis' phone number. I scribbled it down and then gave instructions for a message to be delivered to her room. I left them my number, and the person promised to deliver my message to her right away.

When I hung up, I dialed the number, but got an error saying it was disconnected. I tried it again, dialing more carefully. When it wouldn't work, I called the ship once again, figuring I either I'd made a mistake while writing it down or they'd given me the wrong number. While I waited on hold for a long time, Kylie's doctor came in the room, so I hung up to hear his latest assessments.

I called back later when the staff was preparing for the next group to board. When the person I talked to checked, the number I had tried was correct. That was the only number they had for her. I hung up worried, but sure that she would call as soon as she got my message. She was probably busy getting off the boat and catching her flight. She might have even been in the air and not able to call. I checked my phone throughout the day, but got nothing from Alexis.

I finally decided to go home and get some rest, but first thing the following morning, I showered and got online. I searched for her name on every social media site I could find, but after sorting through tons of Alexis Hales, I didn't see her. She had to be online, didn't she? Maybe I was so tired and my mind was so fried that I'd missed her profile. I decided to try again later when I could think straight and hoped that she would call or text soon.

10

ALEXIS

I woke too early, but couldn't fall back asleep so I finally decided to just get up. There was no reason to stick around for breakfast; I wasn't going to eat, anyway. I packed my things and went down to the deck where disembarking would take place to see if I could leave the boat early. There was nothing else for me onboard and I wanted to get away from there as soon as possible.

Even as I walked through the ship, I saw places Cooper and I had gone to eat, stopped to see the view or walked through. Too many memories that now caused pain. How would I tell Hailey what happened? What would she say?

I waited in line to get off the boat and tried to think of other things. When I got home, what would

I do? Besides seeing my friends and clanmates and family, I would keep looking for a job. I didn't know if I could return to the area without it being painful. Or maybe if I'd returned, I'd somehow find him. I did know which park he worked for, so it couldn't have been that hard, could it? But did he even want to be found?

I didn't know what to think. I didn't want to believe Becca, of course. But Cooper hadn't called. I'd left my information for him, and maybe he hadn't gotten it yet, but couldn't he have called the ship and sent a message to me? Or been connected to my room like at a hotel? Wouldn't he have my number from the Ranger program information?

I reminded myself that he'd had an emergency. I couldn't forget that was the reason for him being gone. It wasn't like he'd just vanished. No, something serious enough to make him leave the boat in the middle of the night and not finish teaching his training program had happened. It might have been something terrible. I hoped no one had died. But, whatever it was, was likely taking his time and attention at the moment.

Okay, then. I'd have to be patient—to wait it out, to see what happened, to not make any decisions just yet and to not jump to conclusions. Perhaps I'd get home, he'd call, everything would be fine and dandy and we'd pick up where we left off. Perhaps he'd been just as upset over not getting to say goodbye as I had been.

Or perhaps Becca was right and he was on to his next fling.

The excitement of traveling had left me. Going home usually wasn't as interesting as leaving, but that time, it was even more difficult. I sat on the plane, blankly staring out the window, trying not to think. I walked through the airport aimlessly, just thinking about my connecting flight and nothing else.

When I landed in Florida, a tiny spark of excitement filled me as I headed toward where Hailey would be waiting. I was still glad to see my sister. When I told her what happened, she said exactly what I thought she'd say: to just see what happened. And that night, she took me out so I could get my mind off things.

But hours turned into days. I had to make a decision about Alaska. If I was going to accept the job, I'd have to go in a few weeks. I kept telling them that I hadn't decided yet. How long would that work before they said 'thanks anyway'?

I hunted for other jobs to see what was available

to me as the days turned into weeks. After the first week, I was able to convince myself that Cooper might still call. If someone had died, there would be a funeral and arrangements to be made and so on. It might take some time for him to get my note from the ship. It might take some time for him to call.

But when one week became three, then four, I knew that was it. I wasn't going to hear from him. In a month, surely the emergency, no matter how difficult, had passed. Surely, he would have found a few minutes to call me or the cruise ship to get my information. Surely, my note would have found him by now. I had to accept the reality that I was not going to hear from Cooper again.

As I came to that conclusion, my heart was heavy. I'd been having stomach aches over all it, losing sleep, and generally not feeling well. When it started to affect me every day, I knew I had to make a change. I headed to the gym, gave myself permission to cry over Cooper one last night, and moved on. It had been great, but it was over. I let him go and went about my life.

But then, the ill feeling didn't fade. I felt emotionally better, but physically worse. When the time came for my period to start and it didn't, the nagging thought in the back of my mind got louder. *What if...?*

When my period was seven days late, then eight, I had to know for sure. I didn't think there was any way I could have been pregnant. I thought back to our night together. Surely, we'd used protection, right? But thinking about it, trying to recall all the details, I remembered that no, we actually hadn't. We'd been so wrapped up in each other, so passionately excited to be together that we hadn't paused for that little bit of precaution. But still. I couldn't have really been pregnant. There was no way.

I purchased a test and took it home where it sat on my bathroom counter for over an hour. At first, I couldn't pee. Then, I realized that I was freaking myself out and that's why I couldn't. I tried to calm down, drank a lot more water, and finally felt the urge. I dipped the stick in according to the directions and set it down. I couldn't make myself look at it. What if it were positive?

I called Hailey instead. "I need you to come over right away."

"Okay, what's going on?"

"Just get over here now!" I hung up and paced, waiting for her.

When she knocked on my door, she didn't look happy. "What's up with you?"

I pulled her arm to bring her inside faster and led her to the bathroom. "I need you to go look."

She put her hands on her hips. "Did you call me over here to kill a spider?"

"What? No!" I shook my head. "The pregnancy test. I need you to check it."

Her mouth hung open and her eyes widened. "The what!"

"Just. Go. Look." I gritted my teeth and pointed.

She went into the bathroom and came out a moment later. She looked at me, her bottom lip worrying between her teeth.

"Well?!" I shouted at her.

"It's...positive."

"No!"

I dashed in and snatched up the stick. Sure enough, two lines were visible. I blinked and rubbed my eyes, willing the extra line to fade.

"This can't be right," I said, the panic making my voice shaky. "This can't be happening. The father wants nothing to do with me! How can I possibly have his freaking baby?"

Hailey put her hands on my arms. "Okay, sit down. Let's just breathe."

She sat me on the couch and got me a glass of water.

"You don't have to decide anything right away," she said. "But you do have some options, here."

"Options."

"Yes."

"I don't have options! My life is over now!"

"Um, hello twenty-first century woman, your life is not over. You're having a baby. It's not the end of the world."

I burst into tears and covered my face with my hands. "I can't have a baby," I muttered through my sobs.

"Then you don't have to." Hailey held me close and rubbed my back. "You'll need to take time and really think this through. You do have options. Several. You'll have to decide what's right for you. If you don't want a baby right now, then don't have one."

"But how could I just...get rid of it?"

"Well, you don't have to do that, either. You could have it and give it to a loving couple who wants a baby."

"But just give my baby away? Then I'd always be wondering, wanting it."

"Then keep it. Be a single mom. Move in with me

and we'll double team it. It can't be that hard to raise a baby, can it?"

I burst into sobs all over again. I had no idea what to do and it seemed that the only thing I was capable of doing was crying. Hailey stayed with me for many hours. She got me fed and made me tea—caffeine free, she pointed out—and made me put on my comfy clothes. We watched a movie together and just hung out.

But when she left that night, I knew I had a decision to make. I took a piece of paper and divided it down the middle, writing 'Pros' and 'Cons' at the top. On the left side, I listed abortion, adoption, parenthood before writing my pros and cons for each.

I'd always wanted children. But did I want them without a partner? I'd never thought I could have an abortion, but did I really want a baby at that point in my life? When I was done, I looked at the list. Each section had several items and no one section seemed to have more than another. I'd been hoping the exercise would help me see clearly what I should do; that the correct answer would have all the pros and few cons and it would be obvious. But no such luck.

The hardest part was knowing I hadn't heard from

Cooper. It was his baby, no doubt about that. I hadn't even thought of being with anyone else but him. Our night together had been the only sex I'd had in more than six months—and was probably all I would have for the next year or so. At least. That was depressing. I thought of what my woman parts would go through giving birth and shuddered. No way could I go through with it. But still, Cooper deserved to know. Even though he might not have wanted to speak to me again, I had to figure out how to get in touch with him.

I called the cruise company again. After being on hold for hours and being passed from person to person, I was told that they could not give me any personal information on Cooper. It didn't matter if it was an emergency. I left my number, but had low hopes that it would get through. If Cooper had my number already and hadn't called, why would he call now, after being given my number again? He'd probably think I was stalking him.

I'd searched for him online a number of times, and then I searched again. Someone should not be that hard to find. I knew his name and where he lived. I knew what he did for a living. I even knew which park he worked for.

When I found the number for the Glacier Bay

Ranger Station, my heart raced. What if I found him? What if I didn't?

When a woman answered the phone, I had a moment of hesitation. She introduced herself as Becca, and I thought her voice sounded familiar.

"Hi, I'm looking for Cooper Hurst. He works for Glacier Bay, but I'm not exactly sure where."

"May I take a message?" she asked.

"Is he there?"

"He's not available at the moment. May I take a message and have him call you?"

I let out a sigh. "Sure. That'd be great." I told her my name and number.

"Wait," she snickered. "Didn't I meet you on the cruise ship a few weeks ago?"

"Yeah. I was wondering if you were the same Becca."

"So, Cooper didn't call you, did he?"

"No, he didn't. But it's very important that I talk to him. Can you please relay that to him?"

"I'll pass it along," she said. "Again. But you know, if he didn't call the first time, I doubt he'll call now."

"I know, but it's critical that I speak with him. Please just tell him that."

"I will, but don't get your hopes up, sweetie; I

warned you about him. In fact, I've already seen him with several women since that cruise. It's probably in your best interest just to move on and forget him."

My throat thickened and I choked back tears. "Please...just tell him." I hung up and broke into sobs.

I didn't know if she told him how important the matter was and he just didn't give a shit, or if he'd moved on. Could he have really just been a player? I didn't know why he didn't call, but he didn't. Weeks went by and I had to decide. I was running out of time.

I was frustrated, confused, worried and lonely. I had to decide the fate of a child. On my own.

11

ALEXIS
ONE YEAR LATER

"Hold still!" I put one hand on the baby's leg to keep him from kicking while my other hand tried to pull up his pants to no avail. He kept kicking, preventing me from getting the pant leg over his foot.

I set the pants down and Kodi looked up at me.

"Well, I guess you just won't wear pants today, then."

At the sound of the knock on the door, I picked him up and went to let Hailey in. She cooed at Kodi and hugged me.

"All set?" she asked.

I held up the baby, who wore a shirt and no pants. "As long as pants aren't required, we're good."

She laughed. "Come on."

In the nursery, with Hailey's help, I was able to get Kodi's pants on and even his socks. Hailey picked him up when we'd finished and cuddled him close.

"What are you going to do without me when you leave?" she asked Kodi in a sing-songy voice.

"Well, clearly, my baby will be only half-dressed, so there's that." I shoved a handful of diapers into the diaper bag and sighed. "I don't know how I'm going to do this alone, but I don't think I have much of a choice."

"I know we've been through this a hundred times, but remember, if it doesn't work, you can come back. I think we were surviving okay."

"Surviving. Barely. Living off ramen noodles to buy diapers isn't what I call living. This job will pay double what I've been making, plus the housing allowance, and they're paying for me to move."

"But it's still Alaska, which is the farthest state away."

"It's always been, Hail. But that's where the job is. Maybe in a few years, when I have some experience, I can move back."

"I wish Owen had been able to get you a job here in the 'Glades. That would have been perfect."

I nodded. "It would have been. But with all the

clans now taking a part in overseeing the park, I think them not having any openings is a good thing."

"Sure. For the park. Not for us."

"Well, no, but I can't change that. Nothing about this last year has been easy. It's not going to be any easier moving across the country with a two-month old and living alone. But I'll be able to pay for daycare, so I'll have help."

"I know you'll do fine." Hailey put a hand on my shoulder. "That's the only reason I can complain so much about you leaving. Because I know you'll do great, even without me. And that kinda sucks."

"Please. I need you more than anyone, you know that. I'm just waiting for you to come visit and fall in love with Alaska."

"I suppose it could happen. But crocs in Alaska?"

I shrugged. I had no answer for that. Hailey had recently gotten engaged to a croc shifter and she was right. Crocodiles were able to live in lots of places, but Alaska was not of them. Adam wouldn't be able to shift much or have the environment he needed. Not like bears, who were more adaptable.

"I still hope that..." I let my gaze fall on Kodi's lips and thought about how much they looked like Cooper's. "Maybe I'll find him. Maybe it'll be different if he knows we have a baby."

"Maybe. But it's a big state."

"It is, but we'll be in the same area. He's a Ranger. The park is big, but not that big; maybe I'll end up working with him."

"Yeah, it could happen." Hailey slung the diaper bag over her shoulder. "Got everything?"

"I think so. At least enough to keep us set until the pod arrives in a few days."

"Then, let's get on with it."

Hailey drove us to the airport where we had a very tearful goodbye. We weren't the only ones crying. Kodi's nap schedule was being interrupted and he wasn't happy about it. But we managed to get on the plane and get to Alaska without too much incident.

Once we landed, I followed my plan. I took the shuttle to the hotel I'd booked. From there, I set us up for our temporary stay. I had an apartment lined up and would go tomorrow to walk through the place and get the keys. Then, the pod would come with the movers and I'd start my new job a few days after that. Within a week, my life would look totally different.

Kodi would start daycare and we'd go there tomorrow, too, to check the place out. I had a long-term car rental booked until I could purchase one with the money I made from selling my old car. It wasn't worth it to have it shipped there; it would be easier to get another car. I didn't think that would take too long, though. In a month, we should be fully settled and enjoying our new life. I just had to tackle day one.

I looked down at Kodi, who sucked on his fist while lying on the hotel bed. "You ready for this?"

He hiccuped, and I took that as a yes.

∽

On the day we arrived, I remember thinking that, in a month, we'd be settled. Well, it'd been a month, but we were anything but settled. I had found a car, Kodi had started daycare, and I had begun working at my new job. All of that was true. I had even gotten the apartment and moved in—only to find out a week later that the entire bathroom leaked and we had to be moved to another apartment in the same building. The landlord had covered our moving expenses and given me a free month's rent for the hassle, but still.

Boxes filled every room. We were not unpacked or settled, so I had to keep looking for things, searching through many boxes to locate the one that contained whatever it was I was looking for. And the car I'd bought had just started making a strange sound and was in the shop. Work had been fine. It was a lot to learn and I felt like I had no idea what I was doing most of the time, but I was getting used to it.

What I really needed were some friends. In everything that had gone on, I hadn't had time to find a clan or really meet people. There were a few people at work who were friendly, and a few were shifters, but I hadn't found a bear shifter there yet. If I could find one, then I could get some information about the clans in the area and hopefully join one. That would give me the support base I desperately needed.

That night after work, I would do something a little different. There was still a little time before I had to pick Kodi up without being charged extra, so as soon as my shift ended, I took off on a run, touring the area, sniffing around, trying to locate some bear shifters.

I'd run for an hour and was starting to give up when I took a left and entered a part of the park I'd never been in before. With a park that was more three million acres in size, that wasn't unusual. The park was so huge, there were tons of Rangers who worked in the same park that I hadn't even met. Everything was divided into sections, and I was amazed at how secluded things were. I hadn't had much time to explore the park to try to find Cooper. Maybe part of me was so hurt, I didn't want to face the possible rejection.

As I ran, I picked up the scent I'd been searching for. It was faint at first, but I followed it until I found a fresher one. Then I found one so fresh, I thought the bear might still be in the area. I ran fast, made a grunting sound to let whoever it was know I was coming, and stopped when I heard signs that someone was near.

I approached slowly so I wouldn't appear to be attacking. When I found the bear—a brown male—I put my head down to show that I was friendly. He dipped his head back and we sniffed each other. I went behind a tree and shifted to human form, staying a bit hidden for privacy. After a moment, he did the same.

"Hi there!" I called out. "Sorry, I don't have any clothes with me." I chuckled.

"No problem. Can I help you with something? You're not from here."

"No, I just moved here. I'm actually looking for a new clan. Are you part of one?"

"I am. And we're always looking for females."

I swallowed hard. What did that mean?

He laughed. "That didn't sound right. I mean, yes, we are always happy to welcome members, male and female alike. We happen to have more men, as does most of Alaska."

"Right." I chuckled, but felt a little uneasy. "Could I meet them some time?" Maybe the rest of his clan was less awkward.

"Well, yeah, sure. We have a meeting tomorrow. You're welcome to come as my guest and meet everyone, to see if it's a fit for you."

"There are some women, though, right?"

"Oh sure. Just more men, is all. I'm sorry, I didn't mean to make it seem like…that just came out wrong."

"It's okay." I started to feel a little better; a little less like he was part of some men's group that sought out available women and hoped to mate them or something.

He gave me the details of where the meeting was and when. I asked if he would mind if I brought my baby along, mentioning he was also a shifter and would need a clan.

"Two for one," he said. "Cool. One thing we don't

have many of is kids, though. I don't know if that matters. We're kind of a young clan."

"No, that's perfect. I could use some friends in the area."

I picked up Kodi from daycare and returned home, wondering what in the world I should look for when choosing a new clan.

12

COOPER

Almost there. I kept running, heading in the direction of our clan meeting. I wanted to make sure I was at least on time, if not early that night. Carson had mentioned he'd be bringing a new recruit and I wanted to be one of the firsts to meet the new arrival.

I'm just glad you managed to bag us a lady! Max said.

Um, there are ladies in this clan already, you know, Kylie piped up.

You don't count. You're the Alpha's sister.

Come on, man, Jace cut in, *don't be like that. It's her first meeting back. Give her a break.*

Thanks, Jace, Kylie thought.

She seems really nice, Carson added. *Has a baby, too, so that'll be interesting.*

A baby? You didn't mention that, I said.

I didn't? Carson wondered. *Sorry. Is that a problem?*

Of course not. It'd be good to get some kids in the mix. We need that.

Yes, we do, Kylie added. *Now **that** might bring more women, Max...*

Really? A baby? Why?

Women love babies, hello? she said.

No mate, though? I asked.

Not that she mentioned.

Sweeeeet, Max said.

Let's make sure we don't bombard her tonight. No hitting on the new recruit, I commanded.

Aw, come on, Max huffed. *You're no fun.*

I saw the building and shifted back as I arrived. First one there. Perfect.

I dressed and set up the room the way I wanted it, then reviewed the list of things I had to discuss. It was our usual monthly meeting where we'd be hashing out clan business, one item being the new recruit.

The others arrived and trickled in slowly. I kept

my eyes on the door so that when the newbie showed, I could greet her right away and make her feel welcomed. But as the time went on, the clan arrived and there was no sign of the recruit.

"Well," I addressed the group, "we're supposed to have a new recruit coming tonight. I don't know if she changed her mind or got lost, but we'll get started and see if she shows."

They murmured amongst themselves and I heard several of the guys perk up at the prospect of a new woman coming in. *So predictable,* I thought, almost laughing. Of course, the idea of Alaska having no women was somewhat of a joke, but in a lot of areas, it was true. Any new blood that came in would surely have no trouble finding a date.

I was about to get to the first item on my list when there was a knock on the door.

Carson jumped up. "That must be her."

All eleven of us had our eyes set on the entrance. When Carson opened the door, I heard someone say, "I'm sorry. I'm not usually late. My car got stuck, but I couldn't run here with the baby." The voice was familiar. My heart jumped.

"It's okay. Come on in," Carson said.

As Carson stepped back, I watched in shock as

Alexis walked through the door, baby carrier in hand.

I let out a huge, involuntary gasp, which caught her attention. Her gaze shot over to mine, and when our eyes locked, she froze. The baby started crying and it took her several seconds to look away and tend to it.

Carson cleared his throat. "So, this is the new recruit I met yesterday…"

My brain failed to function properly. All it could think about was Alexis. *Alexis here. Alexis with a baby. Alexis? Finally? How was this possible? How could she be here?*

Once my brain started to work again, my excitement turned to despair. She had a baby now. She must be dating someone or engaged—or maybe even married. Whatever we had was long over. My throat tightened.

When I hadn't been able to get a hold of her and she hadn't called, I'd known it was over. It had been more than a year since I'd seen her, so I didn't have much hope that she'd turn up or suddenly call. But to see her there; to have her be so close, yet still out of my reach? Knowing it was true killed any shred of hope I'd held onto.

As she found a seat, my despair turned to anger.

Why couldn't she have at least called me? Even if it was to say there was someone else. Or had there been someone else all along and that was why she hadn't called? That must've been it. She was already in a relationship, had come on the ship and had a little fling with me, then went home to him, had his baby, and forgot all about me.

I swallowed my rage and embarrassment. How could I have been so stupid? But there she was. And my clan was waiting for me to welcome her.

I opened my mouth to speak and almost laughed at the sheer irony of it. "Do you want to come up here and introduce yourself?"

She gave me a smile that said she, too, recognized how very much that moment was like our first meeting. Her stumbling in late, coming to the front of the room where I was leading, and talking about herself.

"I'm Alexis Hale," she said, standing much too close to me. "This is Kodi. We're new to the area and looking for a clan to join. I just started working at Glacier Bay National Park as a Ranger."

I felt my jaw tighten. With so many people working at Glacier Bay, I wouldn't have known if she'd been hired by another employee and worked in another area. But to find out that she was not only in Alaska, but worked where I worked, too? I wouldn't be able to escape her.

"Many members of our clan are Rangers in that park as well," I said. "Thank you."

She nodded to me, gave me a strange look, and sat down. I refused to look at her. The anger tore at my stomach, the shame made my neck hot. I felt played. And now I had to look at her and see the evidence of how she'd used me. After she gave me the whole story of being cheated on by her ex and all that? And really, she was the one doing it that whole time? How could I have thought I was falling in love with her? *As if having one ex-girlfriend in my clan wasn't bad enough, now this?* Maybe she and Becca would be good friends and ruin me completely.

Maybe I'd get lucky and she would choose another clan. If she tried to bring in her mate, wherever he was, then perhaps I could convince enough of my clanmates to vote no so that we could keep them out. Having her there was bad enough. Having her there with some other guy's baby was worse, but having her there with a baby and her mate? That would be torture.

I managed to get through the meeting, but by the end, I just wanted to get the fuck out of there. I didn't want to talk to her, I didn't want to see her, I didn't want to feign happiness and say, "Oh, how nice, you have a baby now, congratulations." I didn't want to see her happy if she'd made me so miserable. And I knew someone would ask about it; the way we'd acted toward each other had been too obviously strange. Someone caught it. Probably Jace and Kylie, who knew me better than anyone. But I didn't want to talk about it.

As soon as I dismissed the meeting, most of the group converged around Alexis and the baby. I was able to slip out without notice and took off, running my fastest, wanting as much distance between us as possible. Funny that a year ago, all I wanted was to be close to her. Now I couldn't stand the thought of being near her.

Where are you? Kylie reached out to me a few minutes later. *Didn't see you leave.*

There's a reason for that.

So... Alexis.

What about her?

Is she... I mean, you acted kind of weird. She's not possibly the same Alexis from the cruise last year, is she?

I'd say she's not the same woman I met last year, no. No, she was not at all who I thought she was.

It's not her?

It might be her, but that's not the woman I was with a year ago.

Okay...so it is her. But now she has a baby.

Apparently.

And that bothers you, understandably. But you didn't even talk to her.

Have no reason to. It's just...she played me, Kylie. And I'm sick of this crap from women. If I don't have enough feelings, it's wrong. If I feel too much, it's wrong, too, since apparently, she had someone else the whole time.

You don't know that.

No. But I know that baby's not that old. If she didn't already have someone at home waiting for her, she didn't take long to find him.

She didn't mention a mate.

Her baby has a father somewhere, whether she's with him or not.

Right. She blew out a sigh. *Okay. Heading home. Want to watch a movie with me?*

Not tonight. Thanks.

Okay, bro. Text me later or something.

That night, I got a text from Carson.

Everyone seems to really like Alexis. What did you think? he wrote.

I tapped my thumbs against the screen,

hammering out my response. *I'm not sure this is going to work out.*

Why?

I'll explain later.

I didn't have it in me to hash out the whole thing. I had to figure out my own feelings and work through them before I could discuss the situation with anyone.

As if Carson's text wasn't bad enough, I got another call. I looked at the ID and groaned.

"What do you want, Becca?" I asked.

"You could pretend to be happy to talk to me."

"Why would I do that?"

"Oh, you know, for old time's sake."

"Gee, I'm so happy you called," I said flatly. "What is it?"

"I just wanted to talk to you about the new girl."

"Okay."

"When we vote, I'm not voting for her to join."

I let out a sigh. "I don't even know if she wants to join yet, but what's the problem?"

"Well, for starters, she was flirting with everyone. Everyone. I mean, I get it, there are few ladies and lots of men, and we have a good-looking clan, don't get me wrong. Lots of available men. If it wasn't for me having Ian, I'd date almost any of them. Maybe not Jace. He's too much like you. But, you know what I'm saying."

I laughed. "You have a problem with Jace now, too?"

"Only that he's too close to you. But that's not the point. She's clearly still in love with her baby's father, yet she's flirting with all our guys. She's a player and I'm afraid she's going to cause trouble. Get them all confused, sleep with a bunch of them, cause fights and who knows what else. We have enough drama already. We don't need more."

"She told you who her baby's father is?"

"Yes, she did. She talked about him quite a bit. Like I said, she obviously still loves him. God, she was practically swooning over him."

Her words hit me like a fist to the gut. It was worse than I'd thought. There was a guy, who was apparently still around, and now she was going to come in and mess with my guys' heads? Making them think they have a chance with her, like she did to me? Sadly, Becca was right. If Alexis slept with both Carson and Max, there would be no end to it.

"Thanks for letting me know," I said.

"You're welcome. I just wanted you to be informed. We have an awesome clan. I wouldn't want to see it get torn apart by one female who doesn't belong."

"Noted."

I hung up and tried, as always, to keep Becca from my mind. But her words haunted me; the words that confirmed everything I'd feared.

13

ALEXIS

I got home from the meeting and put Kodi to bed. It'd been a long day, and after the car got stuck, I'd been so frazzled. Then, to see Cooper? I thought my heart was going to stop, then jump right out of my chest. I couldn't believe it. I nearly ran to him and threw my arms around him.

In my mind, I had pictured our moment of reunion. It looked something like us seeing each other, him seeing Kodi and knowing instantly he was his, then taking us in his arms while he kissed me and held me close. God, that wasn't even remotely close to reality. Instead, he looked at me like I'd just keyed his car.

I couldn't understand it. Why had he been so cold to me? He hadn't even mentioned that we knew each other when he had me introduce myself. And hell, if that whole thing wasn't just some kind of weird serendipity...being late again? He would be in front of the room, leading the meeting again? I would stand near him and introduce myself...again? How freaking bizarre.

But that time, the chemistry between us felt like tension—and I didn't know why. Did he have a problem with the baby? Had he moved on and didn't want a girl from his past showing up?

I'd figured we'd get to talk after the meeting; to at least say 'hi' and 'how are you,' to maybe even introduce him to his son. You know, the things people usually did when they hadn't seen each other for a year. But he was gone. Kylie, his sister, apparently, said she hadn't seen him leave.

They had all seemed nice. I could fit in well there and they seemed excited to have a baby and a new person there. But I didn't know if I should try to formally join since it was Cooper's clan. If we didn't talk and there was weirdness between us, how could I be under his leadership? And worse, how in the world would I tell him we had a baby together if he wouldn't even look at me?

When I talked to Hailey that night, she had a different perspective.

"Let's think about this now," she said. "He hasn't heard from you in a year. All of a sudden, there you are. Except you also have this baby. Who looks very much like him. Of course, he knew it was his baby. He freaked out. Can you imagine thinking you're going to your regular clan meeting and suddenly a woman you were crazy over a year ago shows up with your baby? I'd be freaked out, too. And you don't know. He might be seeing someone, so that might have made it worse. Maybe he hurried off to tell her; to break up with her so he could be with you."

"Wow," I said. "I think you're really reaching there."

"You never know."

"What the hell should I do?"

"Well, you found him. No matter what comes of it, you have to at least tell him about Kodi."

"Right. I do have Carson's number."

"There you go. Get Cooper's number and talk to him. That's the only way you'll know for sure. And if it's really over forever, then congrats. You just joined the rest of the world's broken-up couples dealing with shared custody."

Her words brought tears to my eyes. "Right," I whispered, blinking as they pooled and ran down my cheeks. The last thing I wanted was some sort of court order that said when I could see my baby and when Cooper could see him. I'd never pictured that scenario. "I don't think I should have come."

"But you did. You can always come back, but no matter what, you have to tell him."

"I could just leave. Vanish in the night like he did. Pretend it never happened."

"Why would you do that?"

"I don't want to go to court!"

"Whoa. Okay, I know what I said, but you can't assume that will happen."

"It was just so weird that he…he wouldn't even look at me."

"Men are weird."

"Yeah."

After we hung up, I stared at my phone and hesitated. I knew I had to tell him. Whatever I was feeling, it was the right thing to do. I'd want to know if I had a child out there in the world, and surely, he'd feel the same.

I scrolled through my phone and found Carson's number. I texted him, asking for Cooper's number. When he responded, I sighed in frustration at his answer, so I decided to just call him instead.

"Hey, Carson."

"Hi there. Sorry, I just…I'm not sure it's my place to give out that information, you know?"

"I completely understand, believe me. I don't know if you noticed that things were kind of…weird between me and Cooper?"

"Um." He laughed. "Everyone noticed."

"I know him. It's been a while since we've seen each other, and we were both shocked. But I need to talk to him. It's very important. I've actually been trying to get a hold of him for a long time, and this is the first real chance I've had to speak with him."

"Maybe I can give him your number and have him call you."

"I don't know if he will. Please, Carson. I'm not some crazy stalker, if that's what you're thinking. We met on a cruise last year and he had to leave before we could say goodbye. I never had a way to contact him until now."

"A cruise? Wait, that was you?"

"Did he tell you about me?"

"He told everyone about that. Well, I guess it wouldn't hurt. I'll text it to you. Just don't make me regret it."

I laughed. "Definitely not."

When I got the number, I saved it, then stared at it for a long time. How long had I wished for that combination of numbers to be in my possession? How many unknown calls had I answered over the years, hoping it was him? And now here it was. Just ten little numbers that had been keeping us apart all that time. If I'd had that number a year ago, everything would be different now.

I checked on Kodi, then took a deep breath and hit the call button. I figured since he didn't know my number, he wouldn't pick up, so as it rang, I already had a message prepared in my mind. When I heard the phone click and then his "Hello," I panicked.

I hung up and put the phone down. Why had I done that? I shook my head, then dialed again.

He sounded even more wary when he answered again.

"I'm sorry. Hi, it's me, I don't know why I just hung up on you. I freaked out."

"Alexis?"

"Yeah. Hi, Cooper."

"Hi."

There was an awkward silence. Then, I blurted out, "It's been a long time," at the same time he asked, "How did you get my number?"

"Carson. But I had to coerce him for it, so please don't blame him. I'm told I can be very charming when I want to be."

He harrumphed and it made my heart tighten. What had I done to make him hate me so much?

"So, I called because I was hoping we could meet to talk," I said.

"I don't know if that's a good idea."

"The way we left things...please, I just need a few minutes."

"Will you bring your mate along?"

"My mate? What made you think I had a mate?"

"You have a baby."

"Uh, well, a mate's not required to have a child." Was that the problem? He just thought I was with someone and giving me the cold shoulder as a result of his jealousy?

"You're not seeing anyone." It wasn't really a question, more of a statement.

"No. Are you?"

"I don't think that's any of your business."

I huffed. "But it's your business if I am?"

"You're the one who just showed up, who walked into my clan meeting wanting to join, and who is calling me to meet up."

"I never said for sure I wanted to join."

"Whatever. You probably shouldn't."

I swallowed more tears and managed, "Will you

please just meet with me for a few fucking minutes to talk?"

I think it shocked him to hear me speak like that. I couldn't help it, though. What was his problem? I just had to tell him Kodi was his and be done with it. I was tempted to just do it over the phone, but I figured—maybe wrongly so—that he'd want to see his baby.

"When?" he asked after a long pause.

"In an hour? At the visitor center lodge?"

"Fine."

I stared at my phone in disbelief. He'd just hung up on me.

Kodi stirred from his nap and I went to get him up and ready to go.

"Well, buddy, you're going to meet your daddy today. Don't get your hopes up too high; I think he's upset with Mommy." Kodi made a gurgling happy sound as I nuzzled my nose into his belly. "But he'll love you. How could anyone not? You're absolutely perfect."

14

COOPER

My heart was in my throat the whole hour before I was supposed to meet her.

So, no mate. Okay, that was better.

Maybe.

It didn't answer the question of whether she'd had a mate or not when we were together. It didn't answer the question of whose baby it was, or where he was now.

If we were both single... Hope fluttered in my chest at the thought. *Could things be like they'd been before?* Then I remembered the baby and knew it would be impossible. Whatever the case was, there was another man involved now—and according to Becca, Alexis still had feelings for him. Even if they weren't together, she was still hung up on him. And the headaches that came with that? I didn't know if I could deal with it.

I thought back through my teenage years. They hadn't been easy. I had to watch my parents divorce and then my dad remarried. His new wife had a young daughter and I remember how strange it was. There was that kid there all the time with my dad. She was sort of my and Kylie's sister, but not really. He tried very hard to get along with her, but there had been so many issues: problems with the ex-husband, problems with the child support, problems with the schedule. We could never do anything because of her dad. And Kylie and I never really got along with her or developed any sort of closeness. My dad ended up divorcing that woman, too, and married again—that time, sans kids.

I didn't want that life; I didn't want to be beholden to someone else's plans. We would never be able to move away. Maybe that's why she moved back. Could the guy be from Alaska? She couldn't have left Florida with the baby if he was there, so he must be here. How in the world had that happened? Maybe she had come back after the cruise. Maybe even to find me? No, that was too much to hope for.

My brain hurt from trying to think it all through.

When I pictured just Alexis, there was some hope; some excitement, even. But when I pictured Alexis with a baby, all hope sank. I didn't know if I had it in me to love another man's baby. To have to deal with the hassle of that other presence all the time. I wasn't usually a jealous person, but everyone had their limit. If I had to look at the baby and see someone else's eyes, would I really be able to love it like my own?

I didn't take much stock in what Becca had said about Alexis flirting. I doubted it was true, and even if it was, it was likely just Alexis being her friendly, outgoing self. She'd always been good at talking to people, and some might think she was flirting when she wasn't. What I didn't want, though, was to watch members of my clan date her. And if they wouldn't date her because of me, was that fair to her?

I parked at the lodge and shook my head. *This is just to talk*, I reminded myself. *Maybe it's about the clan. Maybe she wants nothing to do with me, and the idea of us being together is the furthest thing from her mind.*

I steadied myself and headed into the lodge. Not surprisingly, she was already there, seated at a table, holding the baby. I walked over and took a seat. "Hi."

She nodded and gave me a small smile. "Thanks for coming."

"Sure." I tried to avoid looking at the baby. It was hard enough to look at Alexis. After a moment, I just stared at the table.

"So, can we go back for a minute, to the cruise?" she asked. "What happened?"

I trained my gaze on a tiny hole in the fabric tablecloth. "My sister, Kylie—you met her—got into a bad car wreck. I left in the middle of the night to be there with her."

"We were told you left because of an emergency, and I get that. But why didn't you ever call me?"

"I *did* try. I called the ship the next day to get your number, but the number was no good. Why didn't you call me?"

"I didn't have your number or a way to get a hold of you. I left my number with the instructor who filled in; Becca something, I think it was. She knew you and said she'd give you my number, but that I shouldn't count on you calling. Then, you didn't. I even called the park weeks later and left my number again with the same Becca."

I looked up and met her gaze. "What?"

She looked confused. "What do you mean, what?"

"You left your number with Becca? Twice?"

"She was filling in for you and was the only link I had to you at all. The cruise company wouldn't give me your number; believe me, I tried many times. When I called the park, she said you weren't available."

I drew my eyebrows together. "Didn't the cruise staff give you my message?"

"What message?"

"Before you even left the boat, they were supposed to deliver a message to you with my number."

She thought for a minute. "I got off the boat early..."

As we looked at each other, the details slowly filling in, our expressions softened.

"Oh my god," she said. "You tried to call me! You left your number and I didn't get it because I got off the boat early? Are you kidding me?"

"I thought...you didn't want to call me."

"I thought you didn't want to call *me*! And after what Becca said..."

I had forgotten about that part. "What exactly did she say?"

"That you were a player. That I was just a fling and that's what you did. And that you never called after you slept with someone. When I spoke with her for the second time, she said you'd already been with several women since the cruise."

I gritted my jaw, sending pain through my teeth. "Do you remember the ex I told you about?"

"The one you had no passion with?"

I nodded. "That's Becca. What I didn't really get into was how she reacted when I ended things. It wasn't exactly the most pleasant break up."

"Wait. Is that the same Becca...?"

"That you met last night?" I offered. "She dyed her hair. Used to be lighter blonde."

She gasped. "I thought she looked familiar! I guess she didn't remember me."

"Oh no, I'm sure she did. She also mentioned that she'd talked to you last night after the meeting."

"I talked to a lot of people last night. Except you. You took off."

"Yeah." I breathed out a huff. "I was pissed. And then when Becca called me later and told me how you'd been flirting with the other clan men, I was even more pissed. And then she told me all about your baby's daddy and how much you still seemed to be in love with him."

Her eyes widened and she paled. She stared at me, hard. "She told you all that?"

I nodded.

"The thing is..." she looked down, then wiped a tear from her eyes. "I am still very much in love with Kodi's father. I didn't realize it fully until I came here."

"So, where is the father? Who is he?"

"It's kind of a long story..."

"Now's your chance to tell it."

15

ALEXIS

A smile spread wide across my face, hitting my eyes. Everything suddenly seemed different. He had tried to contact me. It sounded like he'd been just as upset as I'd been, just as eager to make contact—and had also been just as foiled. I could've killed Becca, but that would be an issue for another time. For the time being, I enjoyed the light feeling in my heart.

He'd just assumed I was with someone else. But he must have been figuring it out, noticing how much Kodi looked like him and realizing how he got his name. He had to.

I let my smile grow and started telling Cooper about Kodi's father.

"Well, the thing is, Kodi's father is amazing. He's

sexy. Funny as hell. We had this crazy sort of whirlwind romance, like what's shown in books and movies, you know? We met and there was instant attraction. There was this fiery passion between us, and we spent every second together that we could. We had a short time with one another, but it was the most amazing few days of my life."

I kept watching him as I talked. Any moment now, it was going to click, and he was going to get it.

"But something happened and our time ended too soon. Then, he was just gone from my life. I missed him terribly. I did everything I could to get him back, but I wasn't able to. I wanted nothing more than to be a happy family, to have that crazy love we first found."

He pushed back from the table and stood. His face was red, and he barked at me, "You think I want to hear this? You think I want to hear all about you and some other guy? The father of your child?"

"Coop—"

"No." He held out his hand. "I've heard plenty. You can just take your little fantasy back to Florida or wherever your dream man lives and—"

"He's here."

"Fine, then go off and be with him. God, Alexis, I thought I loved you once. You really think it's appropriate to come in here and say all this to me? Maybe Becca was right about you after all.."

I sucked in a breath and stood up, too. I raised my finger to point at him and tell him off, but he turned.

"Do *not* attempt to join my clan or talk to me again. I don't want to see you, I don't want to talk to you, I don't even want to know you exist!"

I wasn't so concerned about the fact that I could feel the eyes of other people in the lodge on me as I was that Kodi was now screaming his head off.

Cooper turned back to glare at me and pointed at Kodi. "Will you shut that kid up already?"

He stormed out the door and I turned to pick up Kodi. I met a few eyes and apologized, then sat back down, trying to calm myself. My mind ran back through the conversation as I rocked Kodi. Cooper's shouting had probably been what had upset him. *Nice way to meet your father*, I thought.

I packed up our things and went out to the car, where I sat for a moment before the tears started. How could that conversation have gone so wrong? I was trying to be cute. Trying to be romantic, even, and let him know I still had feelings for him.

I had assumed he'd figured it out. I thought he already suspected Kodi was his just by looking at him and calculating the date. But no, that was asking too much. He probably didn't know how old Kodi was, so he wouldn't have figured out the timeline. In fact, he had barely even acknowledged Kodi, so he most likely didn't notice the resemblance. And as far as figuring out Kodi's name, well that one was less obvious, anyhow.

I'd pictured a grand romantic gesture, where he'd realize I was talking about him, would take me into his arms, and all would be well. How stupid. Just like the dumb dream I'd had all the time. What did I think, that Cooper was going to swoop in and be part of our lives? That we'd somehow be able to rekindle what we had? One thing was clear, Cooper was very different off the boat. Maybe I was, too.

I called Hailey on my way home. "I'm coming home. You're right, we'll figure out how to make it work. I'll get two jobs if I have to."

"Whoa, whoa. What happened?"

I recounted the conversation I'd had with Cooper, and she blew out a long breath.

"Okay. I can see why you'd be upset over that. But, the thing is, he obviously didn't figure it out. Yes, I'd think he would have, but he didn't. So, all he heard was you talking about some other guy."

"Yeah. You know what else? He said he almost loved me once."

"Ugh. Hunt him down and just blurt it out. I know you were trying to do something special and it went horribly wrong, but the only way to fix it is for him to hear the real and whole truth. Then you can decide what to do. But as of right now, all you've done is tell him how amazing Kodi's father is, and he thinks that's some other guy."

I parked my car and rested my head on the steering wheel. "How did I manage to screw this up so badly?"

"You'll fix it. I know you will."

I didn't think calling Cooper would be a good idea. If he hated me so much, it'd be hard to get him to answer. I didn't want to be so lame as to tell him through text or a voicemail that he had a son.

Then I thought about Kylie. She had given me her number. A few other members of Cooper's clan had, too, but being his sister, Kylie might be my key.

I scrolled to her name and called. "Hi, Kylie? This is Alexis."

"Oh. Hi."

"Have you... talked to Cooper recently?"

"Um..."

"So, that's a yes. Okay, here's the thing. I desperately need your help."

"Okay...?"

"I have to tell you something, but I need you to promise not to tell Cooper until after I talk to him. I'm telling you because you're his sister, and he said he wants nothing to do with me, but I have to talk to him. I screwed up big time, and I don't know what to do."

I started crying, despite myself. The whole situation was too much for me.

Her voice was soft when she spoke again. "Tell me what?"

"Cooper is...Cooper is the father of my son. I tried to tell him today and I was trying to be cute about it, but my plan went awry and now he can't stand me. I don't know what to do."

She started laughing hysterically. "You're kidding me, right? Are you serious right now?"

"Yes," I said through my sniffles.

"Come to my house. Right now."

She texted me the address, and I drove over there. I didn't know what to expect, but when she answered the door, she threw her arms around me.

"God, Alexis, what a mess." She helped me with Kodi and got me seated in her living room. "I can't even…I just can't even wrap my head around how the two of you managed to so completely miss every part of this. Yeah, I talked to him just before you called. He told me about how he left his number but you didn't get it, and how you left your number but he didn't get it. I mean, could fate have been any more cruel? Apparently, yes, because a baby happened." She paused to look over at Kodi. "That means he's my nephew!" She reached out her arms, and I gave him to her. She took a moment to cuddle him. "Sorry, that just hit me. I have a nephew. And he's super cute. And God." She held him back for a moment before hugging him close again. "I can't believe we all didn't see how much he looks like Cooper. Look at this."

She took off and I got up to follow her into the kitchen. On her fridge was an old photo of two little kids. One was a baby, the other a boy, a few years old. And the boy looked like Kodi would in a few years.

"That's Cooper?" I asked.

She nodded, smiling. "So you came here, not knowing that Cooper was at Glacier Bay and happened to find his clan? Fate! Ahh! And then when you finally get the chance to tell him, he thinks you're talking about some other guy the whole time. Geez. I can't imagine." We went back into the living room, and she pointed to an album on a shelf. "Look in there."

I flipped open the book and saw Cooper's baby photos. I knew Kodi had looked like him, but seeing the resemblance now was uncanny.

"So, I texted Cooper," she said. "He'll be here in a few minutes."

"Oh." I set the book down and smoothed down my shirt.

"You look gorgeous. I can't believe this. Just crazy." She was still muttering about how insane it all was when someone opened the door. "In here!"

Cooper walked in and froze when he saw me and Kodi. Kylie smiled and handed the baby to Cooper. "I'll leave you guys to it."

She left the room and Cooper stood there, awkwardly holding Kodi.

16

ALEXIS

"What's this all about?" Cooper asked.

I stood in front of him. He handed Kodi to me, but I held up my hands and shook my head.

"Cooper." I took a deep breath. "Look at Kodi."

He glanced at the baby.

"No. *Look* at him."

"Okay?" He looked again, slightly longer that time.

"Do you remember the name of the island we ran to on our last night together?" I asked.

"Kodiak Island?"

"Kodiak? Kodi? A little similar, no?" I looked at him, waiting. How much more obvious could I be? Okay, so I would have to spell it out. "Cooper, Kodi is your son. I named him after the place he was conceived. I've been looking for you for over a year, partly to tell you that we have a baby."

His face slowly fell into complete confusion. I could almost see his mind working. I knew he was a smart man. Why was the concept so difficult for him?

"I didn't get to finish telling you my cruise story," I went on. "When I got home, I waited to hear from you for weeks, thinking you had my number. I remembered Becca saying you wouldn't call, but I never believed her. Until you didn't call. Then I started to feel sick, took a test, and sure enough..." I gestured to Kodi. "When I found out I was pregnant, I did everything I could to find you. The cruise company wouldn't give me your number, even though I said it was an emergency. I couldn't find you online, and I couldn't get in touch with you at work. It was like you were a ghost. I started to think I'd dreamt you up—except I had this little baby who looked so much like you.

"It was hard being a single mom, even with Hailey's help. Then I got a call from some program related to the cruise program we were a part of. They offered me this job on land. It would pay a lot more money than I'd been making, plus a housing allowance. I couldn't turn it down. And I kept hoping that somehow, we would find each other. That if it was meant to be... And then the first bear shifter I came across ended up being your second in command."

Tears filled my eyes. "What are the chances of that?" I wiped them away, but they kept coming. "And then you were so cold to me, I didn't know what to think. I thought you would see the resemblance or figure out the timeline. Earlier, at the lodge? I was trying to be cute. Obviously, it didn't work, but I thought for sure you would know I was talking about you."

The confusion left his face, and he blinked at me. "But you said you were still in love with Kodi's father. *Still?*"

"We'd only known each other a few days. I wasn't going to come out and say I loved you just yet. That would have been a little crazy. But that love didn't fade just because we lost contact. Your memory was alive and having Kodi—a constant reminder of our time—it built that love and those warm feelings. Even if, in the back of my mind, I still thought that you didn't want to call me."

"I did, though."

"I know." I stepped closer and put my hand to his

face. "Kylie said something about fate being cruel. It seems like everything has been working to keep us apart, yet somehow, we found each other again."

"So, just so I have this right." He looked pointedly at Kodi, then back at me. "We both left our numbers for each other, but neither of us got them."

I nodded.

"We both wanted to continue a relationship, looked for each other, but couldn't find any leads."

I nodded again.

"That whole time, we both still had feelings for each other, and meanwhile, you were carrying our baby." His voice broke a little when he said, "Our baby."

I pressed my lips together.

"And now you're saying you've loved me this whole time, and you're here, with our baby—my baby—and...? And what, exactly?"

I shrugged. "I don't know. I'm here. He's here. You're here. That's more than I've ever been able to say before, so I don't know."

"But you love me? Is that what you're saying?"

I laughed. "Yes, Cooper. I love you. I have loved you, probably since the first—well, maybe second—day we met."

He looked at me for a long time, and as I

watched him, his eyes slowly filled with tears. "We have a baby."

He reached out his other arm and pulled me into him. He kissed my forehead, then Kodi's.

"Oh my god. We have a baby. I have a *son*." He broke the hug to wipe at his eyes again.

"Here, I can take him, so you—"

"No!" He held Kodi closer, then chuckled. "I mean, it's okay. I want to hold him." He looked down at Kodi like he was seeing him for the first time. "He does look a lot like me."

"I know. And he'll grow up to be just as good looking as his daddy is."

Cooper looked at me and gave me a slow smile. "All that in the lodge…"

"I was talking about you, silly."

He shook his head. "How did we manage to make such a mess of this?"

"I don't know, but I sure hope we can fix it."

He nodded, then laughed. "Well, I guess there's no voting on you joining the clan or not. Children are automatically accepted into a clan. And you are, too. If you want to be, that is."

I nodded. "I want to be. I don't know what this is, really. I didn't come with many expectations."

"Do you want to be with me?" he asked.

"Do *you* want to be with *me*?"

"Well, I'm not going to let some other guy come in and raise my baby, that's for sure."

"So..."

"We have a baby. We should be a family. Don't you agree?"

"Yeah, but..."

"What's wrong?" he asked.

"I don't want to be together just because we have a baby. That's what you did before, with Becca, isn't it? You were with her because you'd been together for a while, even though there was no love there."

"This is totally different."

"Because we have a baby? People have babies all the time and aren't together. I don't want to be with someone who doesn't love me for me; who wouldn't want to be with me if we didn't have a baby."

He let out a frustrated growl. "Okay. First, I think we need some sort of plan to just be blunt and honest with each other all the time. It's like we keep misunderstanding each other."

I pulled my eyebrows together.

"Alexis, I've been crazy about you since you first stumbled into my classroom. I've longed for you over this year so much, I can't even tell you. I thought I was the one with stronger feelings and that's why you never called. I thought I didn't mean as much to you as you did to me. So, when you stumbled into my life again, very much in the same way, except this time, in front of my clan and with a baby, it stirred up all those feelings again. Except that with the baby, I assumed a lot of things I shouldn't have. And I listened to Becca, which I shouldn't have." He took a moment to glare. "I'll have to talk to her. But the point is, I was only cold, as you said, because I thought you'd moved on. I thought we could never be together, and I was insanely jealous of this man who came along and gave you a baby." He laughed. "I had no idea I was being jealous of myself. I wanted to be that man to you so badly all along. And now, here you are. And here Kodi is, and it's just..."

"Crazy," I offered.

"Crazy," he agreed. "But the point is, I do love you. I've felt that passion we had on the ship every day since then as a deep longing in my heart. I want nothing more than to be with you. If we didn't already have Kodi, then I'd want to marry you and get busy making Kodis. But we do, so we have no reason to wait. Marry me. Today. Tomorrow. Next week. Marry me and be mine forever, no getting away this time."

I laughed. "There's one thing I have to do right now."

He raised an eyebrow at me.

"Can I see your phone?"

He handed it to me with a skeptical look. I went to his recent calls and found my number, then saved it with my name, email, work number, and address. I added Hailey's number and address, then my parents' info before I gave the phone back to him.

"Now you'll always have a way to contact me."

He glanced through his phone, smiled at the additions, then held out his hand for mine. He awkwardly typed with one hand while still holding Kodi, who'd now fallen asleep.

When he handed it back, I saw that he'd entered his address under the contact I'd made for him, and added info for Kylie, his mom and stepdad, and his dad and stepmom.

"Okay," I said. "So, now what?"

"Uh..." He looked at me questioningly.

I waited for him to say more.

"I... kind of asked you something?" he said, rubbing the back of his neck.

"Wait, was that an actual proposal? I thought you were just talking about our future."

"I am. And in that future, I want you to be my wife."

"I want that, too."

He chuckled. "So, that's a yes?"

I leaned forward and pressed my lips to his. We kissed like we were making up for every lost moment we'd missed over the last year.

When the kiss ended, I said, "Yes. Though we may need to take some classes or something to improve our communication."

"I love you," he said. "I'm just going to say what I'm thinking from now on and not assume things."

"Good plan. I love you, too."

He kissed me again, until Kodi stirred and woke.

"Maybe we should go back to my place?" I asked. "We can put Kodi to bed..."

He pulled his keys from his pocket and handed Kodi back to me. "Right behind you. I'm not letting you out of my sight."

17

COOPER

I drove too close to her car. I hoped I wasn't making her nervous, but I was unwilling to take any chances. After all we'd been through, I was not going to lose that woman again. I couldn't rightly keep her in my sight at all times for the rest of our lives, but I would do my best to try.

The drive did give me a few minutes to let things settle in my mind. I hadn't talked much to Kylie before we left; she knew we needed time to ourselves. But it was weird not to talk her about what was going on. There would be much conversation at some point, no doubt. She'd already accepted Kodi as her nephew, but she'd be getting a sister-in-law, too. And then there were the parents. Hopefully, my mother would be so excited over having a grandbaby that she wouldn't be too disappointed in me for having him out of wedlock.

My dad would likely give some unhelpful advice about carrying condoms with me all the time. But they would love Alexis and Kodi. No doubt about that. Even if things were tense at first, Alexis would win them all over quickly.

There were so many decisions ahead of me, I didn't know where to start. Alexis probably had it all figured out already; she was good about making plans. We'd have to find a place to live, plan a wedding, all of that and more. I started to feel a little overwhelmed by the time I pulled up beside her in her apartment's parking lot.

We got out and I helped her carry the diaper bag while she carried Kodi in the car seat. I followed her upstairs and had already made the first decision before we walked through the door.

"So, you'll definitely have to move in with me," I said, looking around and setting the bag down.

"It's not that bad." She laughed. "It wasn't like I got to check out a bunch of places before I came, you know. It's cheap."

"For a reason."

"I'm certainly not tied to this place or anything. We can live wherever. I don't really care."

"Huh." I watched her take Kodi out of the seat and hold him close.

"What?"

"I thought you would have had things planned out already."

"Well," she brushed her hair out of her eyes, "all my plans were thrown to the wind when Kodi came along. I've learned not to plan so much. Things change. For instance, I thought when I found you, it would be some grand moment where we fell into each other's arms, and it was supposed to be this glorious reunion. Instead, my car got stuck in the mud—obviously, your clan doesn't drive to the clubhouse often, but you can't make a baby shift, so I had no choice—and you thought there was someone else, and nothing I had planned worked out. Nothing I've ever really planned has worked out like I thought, so what's the point?"

"There is one thing I think we can plan."

"Well, the wedding will take lots of planning, for sure. So will moving and breaking my lease and all that. Gosh, I didn't even think about that. We'll have to tell our families and we need to make a trip to Florida so you can meet my family."

"For now, maybe we can just plan to spend some time together once the baby is sleeping. That's all I meant." I gestured to the boxes along the wall. "Besides, you're already packed."

She gave me a seductive smile. "Oh yeah? What did you have in mind?"

"Something we haven't done in a long time."

I followed her into Kodi's room. It was obvious she'd spent the most time there. No other room in the apartment looked so put together and finished. She'd hung decorations and made it cute with animals all over the place. She lay Kodi down carefully and watched for a moment to make sure he wasn't going to stir.

We snuck out of the room with the baby monitor and sat in the living room.

I took her hands in mine. "I have to say, I am so sorry you've been alone in this. I'm sorry that I didn't give you my number sooner, that I wasn't more careful about making sure we could contact each other. I should have just gone to your room before I left and said goodbye."

She shook her head. "You were thinking of Kylie. It's understandable. She told me a little about the accident. She almost died? No wonder you weren't thinking about me. I wouldn't have wanted you to be."

"I was, though. I wished you were there with me

to make it better. It was the most terrible few days of my life, and they came right after the best few days of my life. I was just spun from it all. But you went through the whole pregnancy and birth and first few months of Kodi's life alone, and I'm sorry for that."

"It wasn't your fault. And I had Hailey and my family to help."

"I'm still sorry it happened that way. I thought... well, so many things I thought were wrong, so it doesn't matter. But I never saw things ending up like this when we first met."

"No? I can't imagine why you couldn't foresee this craziness."

"But, look at what happened. We found each other again. I wish we had never been apart, but I'm grateful that it was only a year. What if you wouldn't have found me until Kodi was older? It would have been terrible to miss all that. At least I have you both now, and we can be a family, and I won't be missing either of you."

"Ever again."

"Ever again, because if you think I'm letting you vanish again, you're nuts," I said.

"I wouldn't try. I mean, I did move across the country partly because you were here."

"And I am so, so glad you did. I guess I'll have to

tell my boss that his recruitment campaign is a success."

"What part of the park do you work in?"

"Up near the preserve," I said.

"We work at opposite ends of the park. With so many miles between us, we might have never run into each other."

"Nah. There's an annual Christmas party and pretty much everyone goes. I probably would have seen you then."

She laughed. "Well, good thing, because I'd hate to think we might have been so close to each other this whole time and not found one another."

"You know what? Let's not think about that. We did find each other." I tucked a piece of hair behind her ear and leaned in to kiss her.

Once we started kissing, all conversation halted. It didn't take long for things to heat up. After a few minutes of kissing, I was pulling my shirt off. At first, I thought I was moving too fast, but then she pulled the hem of her shirt over her head, too, and wiggled out of her jeans.

I helped her tug them off and tossed them aside. I sat up a little and took a moment to look her over, to take in the sight I hadn't seen in so long.

She crossed her arms over her stomach. "What are you doing?"

"Looking at you. What are you doing?"

"Just kiss me."

I gave her a questioning look and kissed her, then pulled back again. "What's going on?"

"It's just, you know, I've still got a few extra pounds from Kodi. I want you to remember me how I was."

I laughed and moved her arms to kiss all over her stomach. "Are you kidding me? I see your beauty. And I see where you carried our baby." I ran my fingers over the light, silvery stretch marks in her skin. "These are the most beautiful marks you could have because they mean we have something together that can never be undone."

She put her hand to my cheek. "I almost forgot how charming you are. No wonder I slept with you after only a few days."

I wiggled my eyebrows at her, planting kisses along her neck and bit gently on her earlobe. "Am I charming now?" I breathed into her ear.

"Yes," she moaned as I rubbed her nipple between my fingers.

She flinched slightly when I pinched the firm

nub and then I thought of how she'd fed Kodi. I sat up again. "Is this okay?"

"What do you mean?"

"I mean, can you do this?"

"Well, I'm a little out of practice since it's been over a year, but I think I remember how it goes…"

"No." I shook my head. "You flinched when I pinched your nipple. Are they sore?"

"Oh. A little. They get a lot of use these days."

"Alexis, we don't have to—"

"Oh, yes we do." She sat up to meet me and wrapped her arms around my neck. "I've been wanting you for so long. Do you know how many times I thought about our night together?"

"Almost as many times as I did? Wait a minute. So, you haven't slept with anyone else since me?"

"Cooper, I was pregnant. No." She laughed.

"Oh. Right. Well, good. I haven't either."

She bit along my neck and reached into my lap to rub my bulge. "Then I guess we're both a little overdue."

I hugged my arms around her tightly and picked her up, carrying her to what I thought was her bedroom. When I saw the toilet and shower, I said, "Whoops," and carried her into the next room, laying her on the bed.

"Here for a minute, I thought you wanted shower sex."

"Maybe after. I just wanted to make it more comfortable."

She pushed her panties down and spread out naked on the bed. "Your turn." She pointed to my pants.

I obediently took the rest of my clothes off. But I couldn't help feeling hesitant. I stood there, staring at her, my erection pointing straight ahead.

"Are you gonna let that go to waste?" she asked, pointing to my cock.

I climbed on top of her, and she wrapped her legs around my waist. I took my time, making sure she was really ready. She felt wet and moaned when I touched her, but was that enough?

I played with her for a few minutes, feeling her wetness as I slipped my finger in and out. Was it just me or was she super tight? I swallowed hard and she reached down to stroke me. It felt so good that I paused and let her touch me for a few minutes before she moved me into position. Then I had a thought and pulled back.

"Wait."

"What?" she asked, exasperated.

"Well, we have a habit of getting too...passionate and forgetting to use something."

"Huh?"

"Like a condom or something? We didn't last time. Should we now?"

She lay back and thought for a minute. "The chances of me getting pregnant right now are slim."

"Because you just had a baby?"

"And I'm breastfeeding and my periods are really irregular. I mean, it can happen, it's just less likely."

"So...?"

"Do you want to make sure we don't have another baby?"

"Do you?"

She shrugged and I laughed.

"Well," I said, "everything else has come down to chance and fate. Let's just see what happens."

"Okay. As long as you actually get over here and make love to me. Otherwise, it won't matter what fate wants."

I settled back into place and she grabbed hold of me again. When I was in position, she lifted her hips to slip my head inside her. I pushed into her slowly, making sure there wasn't too much friction happening.

She tightened her legs and thrust her hips up, pushing me deeper inside.

"Are you okay?" I asked.

She moved her hips back and forth. "I will be if you stop looking at me like I'm made of glass and just fuck me."

"Yes ma'am." I chuckled and went about my normal rhythm—almost. I was still being gentle, despite what she said. After a few minutes, she sat up and pushed me back, then climbed on top of me, sliding me back inside her and started riding me hard. I was shocked it didn't hurt her, but if she was the one doing it, I didn't have to worry so much.

I finally relaxed and enjoyed the feeling of her slick walls gripping my shaft. Rocking her hips, she slammed down hard on me; I grabbed her ass and moved with her. She was so hot, it didn't take long for me to get close. "Slow down," I groaned.

She leaned over me and tugged on my lip with her teeth. "No. I want to make you come like you've never come before."

With that, she moved faster and harder, forcing me deep inside her until I was overcome by ecstasy and hit my peak. She cried out a moment later and thrust a few times before stopping.

She lay down on my chest, panting. "I needed that."

"You sure you're okay?"

"I'm more than okay. I've missed you."

"I've missed you, too. So much." I closed my arms tightly around her and held her close, vowing to never let her go.

18

ALEXIS

I awoke to Kodi's cry. I was so attuned to it that it didn't take much more than a whimper on his part to wake me. I hurried into his room so he wouldn't wake Cooper and picked him up.

He stopped crying the moment I held him close. *The little guy must be hungry*, I thought, sitting in the rocker with him. One good thing about sleeping naked was that it made breastfeeding more convenient. He latched on and I watched him feed as I considered the last few days. Cooper was in my bedroom. *There. With me.* It was a dream come true. I'd wanted that for so long and didn't think I would get it. But there he was.

"Daddy asked me to marry him," I told Kodi in a soft whisper. "We're going to be a family, the three of us. Just like Aunt Hailey, grandmom and grandpop are family. And you have other grandparents and your Aunt Kylie. We have a whole new life now."

"And I'm going to make sure it's the best life ever."

I jumped and it was enough to disrupt Kodi. He whimpered, but was quickly appeased once he was able to resume nursing again.

"Sorry." Cooper chuckled. "I didn't mean to scare you. I couldn't help watching and listening to you."

I smiled at him. "I know the feeling. It's how I felt when I saw you really hold Kodi for the first time."

"Kodi...does he have a middle name?"

"It's Cooper," I said sheepishly. "I wanted him to have some connection to you always." I grimaced and told him, "His last name is Hale, but we can change that when we get married."

"Whatever you'd like." He smoothed back a loose piece of my hair.

"I want us all to have the same last name. Don't you?"

"I'd be honored to give you both my name."

"And I'm honored to have it."

He kissed my forehead. "Anything I can do to help?"

"Well, once he's done eating, he'll need a new diaper."

Cooper nodded. "Sure, I can do that."

I stifled a giggle. "I'll show you."

When Kodi was finished, I burped him, then walked Cooper through the whole diaper-changing thing. "It was so awkward at first," I admitted. "But when you do it a bunch of times a day, you get good really fast."

"You make it look easy."

I winked at him. "It's not hard. You just love them and give them what they need."

"But how do you know what they need?"

"The same way you know what I need. The same way I know what you need."

I stepped closer and rested my head on his shoulder.

"I need you," he said. "Forever."

"And you have me."

19

COOPER

It felt like I hadn't left the house in weeks. It'd only been a few days, but coming out into the real world after being locked away in a love cocoon with Alexis and Kodi was a rude awakening. But, life had to go on. I'd managed to get us both a few days off when I explained to my—our—boss what had happened, but we had to go back to work eventually. And there were a few other matters that I needed to take care of, too.

I'd helped Alexis get Kodi ready, and we dropped him off at daycare together. I had no idea a baby required so much time and stuff. But I was learning fast and paying attention. I dropped Alexis off in her part of the park, then drove to mine. But lunch was where I had plans I hadn't told Alexis about. I told a little lie that I hoped she wouldn't be angry about later.

I said I was so busy catching up after being off for a few days that I couldn't have lunch with her like we'd planned. Instead, I jumped in my car the second after I punched out and drove straight to the jewelry store. I didn't know much of what to look for in a ring, but I thought I knew Alexis well enough to find something that would work. I took forty-five minutes of my hour long lunch to decide. By the time I walked out of there, I felt confident that I'd chosen well.

We finished our work day, and I headed out to pick up Alexis. When we picked up Kodi, I felt a strange sensation; something like pure wonder and joy at what had suddenly come into my life, and how everything had changed. It was the very best sort of craziness I could ever imagine.

That night, we headed to the clan clubhouse. Alexis was right. We had to at least gravel the main road leading there. My car was a bit better suited to not getting stuck, but I had to drive carefully.

When the clan arrived and the meeting started, I said, "We have two main things to discuss tonight. One, I just realized, and the other is the primary reason for this meeting."

It was still weeks from when we'd have our monthly meeting, but we often had additional gatherings to go over certain matters or to just hang out and get together. We weren't just a clan, we were friends. We were family.

"We need to gravel the main road. I know we all run here, but for those of us who can't, mainly Kodi, we still need to be able to drive. I'm concerned that if we let it go for too long, it'll be costly to fix."

"I can get gravel cheap at work." It was Ian, Becca's boyfriend, who spoke up. He worked in construction.

"Perfect. And as for the more important matter of the night." I held out my arm to Alexis and she and Kodi came to join me at the front. "I know most of you have heard by now, but I want to officially introduce my fiancé and son."

The room erupted in cheers and claps. I waited a few minutes, smiling at Alexis and Kodi as he looked around in wonder.

"I know we usually vote on new clan members, but this is a bit different," I continued when the noise died down some. "Kodi is an automatic member of the clan until he comes of age, when he can choose to stay or leave. As my wife, Alexis will be, too. But I thought, just for tradition's sake, since she's not technically my wife yet, we could take a vote. Anyone in favor?"

They all shouted and put up a hand.

"Anyone opposed?"

No one moved. I looked at Becca to make sure, but she gave an annoyed smile and turned to kiss Ian when she saw me looking at her. Becca knew better than to go against me now. After I'd talked to her—reamed her out, really—about everything she'd done, she confessed to changing Alexis' number in the cruise ship's system, preventing me from calling her, and to throwing away Alexis' number instead of giving it to me. Becca wasn't exactly on my list of favorite people, and she knew it.

"It's settled, then. Our two newest members." I put my arm around Alexis and pulled her close. "There is just one more thing."

I dropped my arm and got down on one knee. She looked at me curiously.

"I already asked Alexis to marry me and she accepted, but it really wasn't the most romantic proposal ever since I just kind of blurted it out."

They all laughed. Most had heard the story by that point, anyway.

"So, I wanted to make up for that." I took the box from my pocket and she gasped when I opened it to reveal a diamond ring. "Alexis, we've been brought together more than once through extraordinary circumstances, and I believe it's because we're meant to be. I want to live an extraordinary life with you and our son, and hopefully many more kids to come. Will you now, in front of all our clan, agree to become part of my life forever as my wife?"

She blushed and looked around the room. "Nothing like being put on the spot, eh?"

The crowd chuckled and she smiled at me. "What do you think, Kodi, should we do it?"

He looked at Alexis, then at me. He leaned forward, reaching his tiny hands out for me for the first time. As his chubby little arms waved in the air, I reached back, proudly taking my son in my arms.

A giant 'awww' erupted from the clan and I blinked back tears. "I think that's a yes?"

"I'd say so."

I slipped the ring onto her finger, and she took a moment to take a closer look at it. "It's amazing," she said quietly to me. "Thank you. When did you do this?"

"Oh." I made an apologetic face. "When I said I couldn't have lunch with you, I was actually out getting your ring..."

"As long as those are the only kinds of lies you

tell me, you're forgiven." She kissed me and showed Kodi the ring.

"Now that that's taken care of," Kylie said, standing from her seat, "we can let the celebration begin!"

Alexis and I exchanged looks.

"You didn't think we'd let you guys get engaged and not throw a party to celebrate, did you?" Kylie put her hand on her hip and grinned. "Party time!"

The clan went into action. Several people went outside to get things they'd stashed out there. They brought in food, a cake, decorations, even a bottle of wine that they gave to us. Kylie handed it to us and said to Alexis, "I called my doctor to check, and she assured me that a glass or two of wine while breastfeeding is totally fine, as long as you don't go getting plastered."

Alexis laughed. "Thanks. That's very...thorough of you. I'll keep that in mind."

Kylie put her arm around Alexis' shoulders. "Oh, I have tons of ideas. We'll have to talk wedding stuff real soon. Mom is so excited, and we'll have to get your family up here to meet everyone!"

I watched Alexis and Kylie walk off to join the party, chatting about dresses and hair styles. *She'll make a good bridesmaid*, I thought. *As long as she doesn't go too overboard.*

I held Kodi and appreciated the moment. My clan surrounded me, celebrating my engagement to Alexis. That alone was miraculous; that we'd found each other again. And then there was Kodi. He came along much sooner than I expected, but I couldn't imagine life without him, even after just a few days.

Fate brought my family back to me, and I couldn't have been more grateful.

THE END

ABOUT THE AUTHOR

Meg Ripley is an author of steamy shifter romances. A Seattle native, Meg can often be found curled up in a local coffee house with her laptop.

FREE BOOK SERIES!

Download Meg's entire *Caught Between Dragons* series when you sign up for her steamy paranormal romance newsletter!

Sign up by visiting Meg's Facebook page: https://www.facebook.com/authormegripley/

Printed in Great Britain
by Amazon